PRAISE FOR ERIKA KROUSE AND
COME UP AND SEE ME SOMETIME

"The stories are full of zingy one-liners that would give West a run for her money, but they never detract from the book's sense of moral and literary heft. With her instinctive grasp of the darkness lurking in the corners of female comedy, Krouse is closer in spirit to Lorrie Moore than Melissa Bank. . . . A frisky and unexpectedly serious first book."

—The New York Times Book Review

"Krouse is a masterful and elegant storyteller, and these tales are filled with narrative and stylistic surprises. . . . Dead-on dialogue, realistically drawn scenes of extreme psychological discomfort, a subtle use of metaphor, and bursts of lyric epiphany: an irresistible debut."

—Kirkus Reviews (starred review)

"Krouse is in the same league as Mary Gaitskill and Lorrie Moore, her fiction wise to the bravado required of Liberated Women throughout the ages."

—Publishers Weekly (starred review)

"Incoherent relationships, other people's weddings, abortions, fear of flying, and loneliness: Krouse astutely ponders them all, balancing pain with mordant wit and a preference, always for freedom."

—Booklist

"Krouse fills her collection of thirteen sharp stories with nervy women worth getting to know."

—Entertainment Weekly

"These stories are smart, funny, and unexpected. There is surprising range here. The patience of the work is beautiful, allowing full appreciation of the craft without calling attention to it."

—Percival Everett, author of *Glyph* and *Watershed*

"Erika Krouse's writing is exquisite—clever, funny, elegant, powerful, wise. I read *COME UP AND SEE ME SOMETIME* and was spellbound. Her stories are of the heart and soul—their compassion is touching, their sharpness terrifying. I gobbled up this book in one sitting—it was like eating a whole chocolate cake. I knew I should savour it, make it last, but it was so delicious, so moreish, such a fabulous treat, I ended up stuffing myself."

—Anna Maxted, author of *Getting Over It* and *Running in Heels*

"Like her muse, Krouse focuses on savvy, sexy women who need loving, but need their autonomy more. Propelled by mordant wit, and an honesty that can sting, these gripping stories sometimes veer into dark territory. Their compressed intensity explodes on impact."

—Emily Wortis Leider, author of *Becoming Mae West*

"Erika Krouse's stories about men and women and all the trouble they cause each other are painfully accurate, relentlessly hopeful, and amazingly funny."

—Daniel Wallace, author of *Ray in Reverse* and *Big Fish*

Come Up
and
See Me
Sometime

—

Erika Krouse

WASHINGTON SQUARE PRESS
PUBLISHED BY POCKET BOOKS
New York   London   Toronto   Sydney   Singapore

This book is a work of fiction. Names, characters, places and incidents are products of the author's imagination or are used fictitiously. Any resemblance to actual events or locales or persons, living or dead, is entirely coincidental.

 A Washington Square Press Publication of
POCKET BOOKS, a division of Simon & Schuster, Inc.
1230 Avenue of the Americas, New York, NY 10020

Copyright © 2001 by Erika Krouse

Originally published in hardcover in 2001 by Scribner

ISBN: 978-1-5011-4272-7

First Washington Square Press trade paperback printing May 2002

10 9 8 7 6 5 4 3 2 1

WASHINGTON SQUARE PRESS and colophon are registered trademarks of Simon & Schuster, Inc.

For information regarding special discounts for bulk purchases, please contact Simon & Schuster Special Sales at 1-800-456-6798 or business@simonandschuster.com

Cover design by Marc Cohen
Photo credit: Plasticstock/Photonica

Printed in the U.S.A.

Some versions of the stories in this collection have appeared in the following publications: "My Weddings" in *The Atlantic Monthly*; "What I Wore" in *Story*; "Other People's Mothers" in *Ploughshares*; "Mercy" in *Shenandoah*; "The Husbands" in *The New Yorker*.

For my girl Meghan

Contents

Endless thanks to Sarah McGrath, Mary Evans, and Daniel Wallace for all their help with this book. Thanks also to the magazine editors who first published these stories, especially Michael Curtis and Will Allison. Big thanks to the Alps Boulder Canyon Inn, the Bread Loaf Writers' Conference, and the Sewanee Writers' Conference. And last, thanks to all my friends for their support.

*Miss West . . . you
are the greatest female
impersonator of all time.*

—George Davis

*It's just lousy enough
to be funny.*

—*Variety* reviewer of
Mae West's
The Constant Sinner

My Weddings

———

I'm single because I was born that way.

—Mae West

My first wedding was Aunt Marcia's second. I wore a straw hat with a baby blue ribbon. The church was like an old schoolroom. Before the "I do," before the kiss, I fainted away in the pew. My mother carried me out the back door, rolling her eyes.

Queasy, I sat on the cement steps. "You'd better not do that at *your* wedding," my mother told me, and spat on a handkerchief to wash my face. I started to cry, because I was confused, and because I had lost my hat. My mother touched my tears with the corner of the handkerchief. "There," she said, "that's a little more appropriate." When I got home, before I even unbuckled my patent leather shoes, I opened the big blue dictionary and looked up "appropriate."

MY FRIEND Pamela liked to play Bride. She was usually the bride, since we played at her house. I was usually the minister.

We had wrapped her head in a bedsheet with lace doilies stapled to it. Her bouquet was green and red tissue paper. She wore her best dress-up clothes—orange beads, and a pink evening gown that trailed behind her. The only trouble was, she kept stepping on it in front. "This stupid thing," she said as she walked down the hallway, while I sang, "Here comes the bride," in my loudest, most celebratory voice.

"Hey," I said as she approached the cardboard box altar. "Your dress isn't white."

"So?"

I tried a different approach. "When can I be the bride?"

"After I'm the bride," Pamela said, adjusting her veil.

I knew that this offer meant nothing. A second bride was no kind of bride.

"Do you take this man to be your awfully wedded husband?" I said in a bored voice.

"I do." Pamela was demure, holding her bouquet lightly in her fingers.

"Kiss the bride."

Pamela kissed the air passionately.

After the kiss, I stood at the altar. Pamela looked at me. The bouquet dangled from her hand.

I suddenly remembered. "Oh—throw the bouquet."

She threw it, and I ran from the altar to pick it up. It withered in my clutch. Pamela's ankle suddenly lopped sideways, and her foot fell out of the large shoe.

"What happens next?" I asked.

SAM VISITED me in September, and I drove him to Rocky Mountain National Park. Sam wanted pictures of elk, bighorn sheep; he wanted a mountain lion. I pulled the car over for every herd of animals. Sam jumped out with his point-and-shoot every time. He paused. The elk stared right at him. The bighorn sheep tossed its big head in Sam's face. One after another, the animals stood perfectly still and then finally leaped away, disgusted, as Sam lowered his camera. "Missed it."

We walked down the street in Estes Park with fresh-bought ice cream cones. "My wife," Sam said, "will be intelligent, educated, and ambitious—yet," with a finger raised, "will want to have approximately five to seven children."

"Bullshit, Sam," I said, hitting his hand as if it were a tennis ball. A penny fell from the change in his grip. He bent to pick it up.

"Does it work the same when it's your penny? Do you get good luck when you pick it up?" I asked.

"No, but I'll drop it again if you like. You can pick it up and get lucky." He dropped the penny. It made a cheap sound on the pavement.

I bent down to pick it up. It was shiny and new. When I straightened up, Sam held out his hand. I put my hand there, and he pulled his away. Then he held it out again. I dropped the penny in the center of his palm. He put it in his pocket.

Two months later he called and said, "I'm getting married. I'm in love. We took a compatibility test and scored way high."

She had the whole wedding planned in advance. Before she even met him. In a laminated pink notebook, with sketches and prices. All the songs, all the special readings by Kahlil Gibran. All she had to add were the initials on the napkins, the name on the cake.

So easy, so few decisions for him to make. He lucked out on a girl like that, I told him.

MY MOTHER called me at my soon-to-be-old apartment the day that Johnny and I were moving in together across town. "The phone'll be disconnected at any minute," I told her, kicking a wad of crumpled-up newspaper against the cabinet door. It bounced back to my toe, and I did it again.

"Don't do it, don't do it." She was crying. "Don't do it."

"We already signed the lease. There's a big orange moving truck outside. Johnny sprained his groin trying to lift the couch with the Hide-A-Bed."

"But what will he think of you? What will he think of me?"

"Mom, he doesn't even know you."

"Put him on the phone."

I argued, but she was silent until I handed the phone to Johnny, who was sweating, holding an empty canary cage.

"Yes, I understand. Yes . . . No . . . No . . . Yes."

He handed the phone back, and I asked my mother, "Okay, what did you say?"

"None of your beeswax."

After we hung up, I asked Johnny what she had said. He said, "I couldn't begin to tell you." But he put his sweaty arm around my shoulder, and told me that he would pack the rest of the truck himself. That I should sit alone for a while and contemplate. That if I had any doubts, to tell him today. Because after today, it was all over.

ALCOHOL WAS served, champagne wreathed with cool white cloth napkins, although this bride was a Seventh-Day Adventist. We knew her through Johnny's job. The day was cold and misty, but heat blowers had been installed in the tents. As I walked too close past one of them, it melted my stockings in one hot blow. I looked down at the strings of mesh, fused together in thin snakes. Johnny laughed and offered me his pants.

A young couple stood at the cake table, drinking nonalcoholic champagne. The woman, who had glasses and a frumpy haircut, smiled a lot. She wore a long angora sweater dress with a matching cardigan draped over her shoulders. Hey, I thought, you're my age. You can't do that.

She said, "I don't know. This champagne doesn't taste nonalcoholic. It's just a little too convincing."

"I don't care," her husband said. "It is what it says it is."

I concentrated on standing upright on the wet earth. But my spike heels sank into the mud, and my shoes kept getting stuck.

"Our wedding had no champagne," the wife said. "So you

couldn't get them mixed up, nonalcoholic and alcoholic champagne. There just wasn't any. Just coffee, tea, like that."

"Are you an alcoholic?" I asked.

"Certainly not," she said.

I was thinking about the word "certainly" and how I rarely heard it in conversation anymore. Then I realized that they probably couldn't drink because of their religion. I slapped my forehead with my palm, while my heels dove into the ground again.

"Mosquito?" the husband asked politely.

She was a marketing manager, and he was an accountant. They worked for the same company and had been married since they were both nineteen.

"And you?" they asked.

"Oh, not much. Part-time sometimes, temporary other times."

"Who are you here with?"

I pointed to Johnny with the bottom of my champagne glass. At that moment he was showing a woman how he could click his heels together in the air. The woman laughed and applauded. Some mud splattered on her shin from the heels of his shoes.

I said, "Johnny there. I live with him."

"Ah," the husband said. "You're married to Johnny."

"No. I live with him."

They nodded. The wife said, "Well, then," and brushed her husband's shoulder. Her long nails made scraping noises on the tightly woven cloth. They moved together toward a couple under a dripping tree. "Oh, Seth, Marie," the wife said.

I stood alone again, holding my glass in my hand. After all, I was what I said I was.

JOHNNY AND I were underdressed for Sam's wedding. Johnny wore a big white shirt and no tie, and I wore a kimono. Nobody talked to us, but a big band was playing, so we drank a lot of wine and headed toward the floor. First we tried a polka, then a jitterbug, then a tango. Johnny pushed me into a bridesmaid's bare back, and I stepped backward, detaching her foot from its satin pump. "I'm sorry," I told her, then whispered to Johnny, "Why can't you lead worth a damn?"

I walked outside. Standing in front of me was a statue of Hiawatha with Minnehaha in his arms. Her dress hung in strips, and his biceps barely bulged under her weight.

I heard Johnny walk up behind me. "See that?" I pointed to the statue. "Is that how it's supposed to be?" I turned around, but it wasn't Johnny, it was Sam, the groom.

"Yeah," he said, "but you take what you can get." We looked through the window at the wedding guests, and at Johnny dancing with the bride. They were beautiful together, the whites blurring together, the bride ringing on his arm like a giant bell. They could have been any two people that you had seen once and forgotten.

"BUT IT wouldn't feel like a wedding if we drove to Vegas and got married by an Elvis impersonator," I said, holding a spatula. "We could act like it didn't mean anything." In the pan, the eggs chugged like a motor.

"Do you really want to get married in Las Vegas?" Johnny asked, next to the stove.

"No," I said, confused. "No, I don't really want to get married."

"Good. Me neither. After Sally, I promised myself never again."

"What if you think about wanting to marry me and I think about wanting to marry you? And we'll both know that we won't do it—that we'll promise not to do it."

"But I don't want to."

"Even with me?"

"What are you talking about? You hate all this. What is it that you want? The wedding part?"

"No. I couldn't stand to be around my family for a whole day."

"Do you want to be married?"

"No. Everyone would expect me to take your last name. Get fat."

"Everyone who?"

"Just everyone."

I had meanwhile flipped the eggs for the second time, so the yolks were faceup and coated with a doughy white film. Johnny turned the burner knob to OFF.

I looked around the yellow kitchen, with the yellow linoleum peeling at the edges.

"I hate yellow," I said.

"Well, that's what you get when you rent," Johnny said. "Listen, honey. I love you. I don't know what you're asking me for."

"I want to be that important."

"To whom?"

I started crying, sliding the eggs from the pan and onto a plate. They had sat too long in the hot pan and were now rigid, even the yolks.

"I want you to want me like that. I want you to love me that much. As much as you loved Sally."

Johnny ran his fingers through his short hair and looked at me blearily. "It wasn't about love with Sally. It was about marriage. It was never about love."

"I still want you to love me that much."

He looked at the plate and then at my face. His voice was scorched and halting. "Do you love me that much?" he asked.

I INTRODUCED Nancy and Gary at an informal wedding reception. Nancy was Johnny's coworker, one of those embarrassing guests who laugh too loudly at everything everyone says. Gary had wispy hair and permanently flared nostrils. He had once followed me home telling me about his pet lizards.

They talked at the buffet table for two hours, after the reception had moved outdoors, after the keg burped its last. Nancy flushed red. Her voice became even louder, her shoulders even wider. She's in love, I thought, and turning into a man.

Nancy finally left after saying good-bye for thirty minutes. Gary stayed, holding an empty plastic cup. "Go after her," I whispered. He hesitated until he saw her brake lights ignite in the parking lot. Then he ran toward her, waving with both arms.

Gary called me the next day. I had been up all night and wore a purple crescent under each of my eyes. Johnny was still in the bathroom, crying. "I was thinking of asking Nancy to coffee," Gary said.

No, not coffee. A date. Say the word "date." "Say 'date,'" I said. "Bring flowers. Kiss her good night, with tongue."

He repeated everything. Date. Flowers. Tongue.

In the next room, Johnny had emerged from the bathroom and was dividing our books into stacks. He got *The Great Gatsby*. I got *Anna Karenina*. *Romeo and Juliet* we gave away, since in that one, both of them died.

GARY TOLD me about his engagement over a hot cup of coffee. The windows were steaming in the coffee shop, and I drew little animals in the frost on the windowpane while he talked.

When Gary proposed to Nancy, it was raining, but he had planned a picnic, so they spread a blanket and sat on a curb. The chicken had gotten soggy, but the potato salad could be saved. He handed her a small white box. Nancy started crying. When she saw that the box contained a pendant, not a ring, she cried harder.

That night they called their parents. His hooted so loudly

that Nancy could hear their voices through the receiver from across the room. Her parents were quiet. They said, "Oh."

When she got off the phone, Gary asked, "How did they feel?"

Nancy said, "They said, 'Oh.'"

Gary slept all night, but Nancy walked back and forth in the moonlight. When the sun came up, he said, she was still waiting by the window. He woke up. She looked at him with her red-rimmed eyes and said, "Okay, I'm ready for it."

"Ready for it?" I asked, suddenly looking away from the window.

"Yeah, I guess she meant that she was okay with the idea," Gary said.

"Is that what she meant?"

"I didn't ask," he said. "Who knows what anyone thinks anyway?"

I PLAYED piano at a Presbyterian wedding, for a friend of a friend. The piano was good, the flowers were fragrant, the dress was misty white. The stained glass was blue.

They looked at each other and cried through the service. They choked on their vows. They said, "Yes, I will." I cried too as they clutched each other and kissed and kissed and kissed.

AT NANCY and Gary's wedding reception, Johnny and I did the wave-salute at each other from our respective tables. He had brought a date; she was blond, drunk, and kissing him. I had no date, but my stomach was the flattest it had ever been.

Johnny asked me to dance. I pulled close to him and smiled at his date.

"I think she's the one," he said.

"The one what?" I asked.

"You know," he said. But I didn't—not really.

I left him alone in the middle of the dance floor and asked someone else to dance. He said no, so I asked someone else. He also said no, looking at his curly-haired date.

Gary, the groom, waited for me at my abandoned table. "Do you want to dance?"

"No," I said, "I want nothing."

"Look at her," he said, and pointed to his bride. So I did. Her dress was enormous—she was packed in like a lace sausage. She thumped someone on the back so hard that his hors d'oeuvre flew out of his hand and dropped to the floor.

"I love her," Gary said, "I love her completely. My love for her is complete."

And it was. Complete. And I wasn't. Completely. Relief and fear tangled together, like the hands of women clutching in the air for a falling bouquet of something.

No Universe

———

"Can you handle it?"

"Yeah, and I can kick it
around, too."

—Mae West

When I heard the news I said, "How can I be infertile when I'm the only member of my family that's ever gone to therapy?"

The doctor pulled off her gloves and said, "Just *probably* infertile. You never know, miracles happen. Are you married?" I shook my head. She said, "Then what does it matter?" She left the room, closing the door behind her. I slowly pulled my feet out of the stirrups.

The rest of the day, I felt different. When I drove back to the office I thought, *Look at the infertile woman in the car, driving a stick shift.* At the supermarket salad bar I thought, *Infertile woman selects a tomato.*

But then I realized, maybe this is the answer. I've always felt secretly disgusted with new mothers. I hate how they say, "I just want to spend all my time at home with my baby." Yeah, and I just want to spend all my time in the Oval Office with Ben and Jerry, but we can't all manage that, can we?

Then there's the way they talk incessantly about their bodies, and what baby eats for breakfast. And that maternity leave, extending indefinitely until they don't know how to run all the latest computer programs anymore.

But that's just rich women, mothers with the luxuries of both money and partner. The rest of them take correspondence courses to finish their mail-order MBAs, when all they ever wanted to do was paint pictures. Or tap dance. Anything but what they're doing now: searching for affordable day care and thinking of creative ways to make peanut butter and jelly sandwiches. Suffering for the sake of the future, which is the ultimate form of procrastination. No way, baby. So to speak. Not me, anyway.

MY FRIEND Mona called me at work. "I forget. Does the rabbit die or not? When you're pregnant?"

"Dies. 'The rabbit died.' Yeah, that sounds right."

Silence on her end while I kept typing. Then, dryly through the receiver, "So what do I have to do? Knit a booty?"

I froze, arms suspended above the keyboard in a Frankenstein pose. "Holy shit."

"Yeah. Shit. Shit."

I turned and my chair squeaked. Mona said, "It's David's. Don't congratulate me. I'm going to 86 it. Will you come? Be the, uh, daddy?"

"Of course. David won't go?"

"David doesn't know. Hey, that rhymes." I didn't say anything. She said, "Oh come on, Stephanie."

"You should tell him."

"Not David. He tells Hillary jokes. David eats bacon for breakfast every day."

"So, he's a little conservative. What do you expect? We live in Colorado Springs."

"He'd make me marry him and have the kid, and then he'd name it after himself."

"Nobody can make you get married, Mona."

"Please." Her voice was thin and far away.

"OK," I said. "We'll do it and then you'll sleep over."

"Like a slumber party. Sort of."

"How are you feeling?"

"All right. Either I'm shallow, more liberal than I thought, or it hasn't quite hit me yet."

"Hey, what if you had the baby and gave it to me?" I actually said this casually. Then I immediately thought about my studio apartment, my big plans to teach English in the Democratic Republic of Congo, how I haven't been able to afford a dentist visit in almost three years.

Mona snorted.

"It's feasible," I said.

"Stephanie. It's mine."

"Yeah."

"No creative solutions. I'm getting an abortion."

"I'll help you."

"Thank you. Just get me through the door."

"It's a simple procedure."

"Easy for you to say."

Then I heard through the phone, "I'm sorry, I'm sorry, I wasn't thinking. But be glad you don't ever have to go through this. Really." Even so, there was something smug in her voice. Or maybe it was tears or food or something like that.

I WALKED Mona across the picket line of men and women shouting in the rain. "Murderers," they yelled. Mona gave them the finger. I did the same. We shared an umbrella above our frizzing hair. All the picketers wore shiny slickers, their bangs plastered to their foreheads.

A wet man in a yellow raincoat shook a jar in our faces. Mona put her hand over her mouth. I stopped and asked him, "If you have so much respect for human life, how can you put it in an old pickle jar?" He silently shook the jar again like a maraca, the fetus rattling inside.

Once we were in the office, the nurses were kind, the doctor was kind, it was over in three hours. Several women tapped their feet in the waiting room. A few men fidgeted or slept in their seats. I read an article about the complex social structure of bees, and then one on Van Gogh's ear. I thought about taking a walk, but it was still raining. I ate three candy bars. I half expected to hear the sounds of a large vacuum cleaner.

I examined the faces of the women as they pushed open the double doors, rejoining boyfriends or rattling their own car keys. They didn't seem happy or sad. They seemed crampy.

Then Mona was standing at the counter, writing a check. She didn't look at me when I put my hand on her back. "How was it?"

She was concentrating on signing her name. She picked up a big pink receipt with procedures checked off in carbon ink and dropped it into her purse. Then she turned to me and sighed.

"Too easy. It made me uneasy."

She looked fine. Pink cheeks, hair a little mussed in the back. I patted it down. She said, "Make a plan for me. I'm whipped." We headed out. As we passed the picketers, Mona waved slowly like the Queen of England, from the wrist.

I've never made the mistake of thinking that everything I do is good. I've chosen badly on purpose, badly by accident. I once made fun of a man who was stumbling across the street, too drunk for walking, nearly too drunk to stand. Then I realized too late that he was in fact disabled or suffering from some incapacitating disease. The smile still trembling on my face like an aftershock. I've been terribly sorry for things unnoticed, for things stopped just in time or nearly too late. For all those choices better off aborted or barren.

How does this fit in? It doesn't, does it?

BABIES WERE suddenly everywhere I went. In the fluorescent light of a midnight search in the grocery store for melatonin, they looked like shrieking Claymation characters, legs banging maniacally against the side of the grocery cart. Or sometimes they looked like those plastic dolls with a string coming out of their backs. There was one lying prostrate at the Koala Bear Kare station in the airport bathroom, laughing every time a toilet flushed. Babies at a distance. Across the street, a pregnant woman pushed a stroller in front of my window every five minutes. Babies on TV, selling diapers, clothes, dog food, even automobiles. Automobiles with car seats.

Somehow it wasn't the same thing when they were already five or six and whining about the long line at the bank, or asking for some ridiculous doll that shaves its own legs. But as babies—heads wobbling on their latex necks, toes wrinkled from sucking, long threads of spit hanging from their soggy lower lips—I couldn't figure out how to feel. So I polled my friends.

"What do you think about when you think about infertility?"

"Nothing," Mark said.

"At all?"

"Well, I think a little bit about my vasectomy."

"You had a vasectomy?" He simultaneously looked both more and less attractive than he had a minute ago.

"After my first marriage."

"Have you ever regretted it?"

"Yeah, when the AIDS thing became a big deal and I had to wear condoms anyway."

"So you have no feelings about infertility itself?"

"No."

"Why?"

"It took human civilization until Christ's time to even come up with the number zero."

"Point, please?"

"What is there to think about something that isn't anything?"

When I asked Amy, she said, "I think about my ovaries. And how you're born with them and all the eggs are already intact. And each of those eggs contains all the eggs of future generations. Like a little universe. So when I think about infertility, I think, no universe. No universe . . . But it's all so academic anyway, I mean, who really gets to experience their full potential?"

Anthony said, "I think about the world population problem and say, hallelujah, Darwinism at work."

Mona said, "Big deal, adopt."

Fran said, "I think about life becoming real exotic. Like, no more working as a receptionist. I think about getting a graduate degree, maybe a cool job that lets you wear the miniskirts that nobody else gets to wear because they all get varicose veins when they're pregnant. Oh yeah, and you can tattoo your stomach. You can live in foreign countries with no health insurance."

Ellen said, "Husband dog sofa."

"What?"

"Those are the three stages of commitment in a woman's life. First she gets married. Then she adopts a dog. When she's really settling down, she finally buys herself a sofa."

"I have a sofa."

"You found it next to a dumpster, Stephanie."

"What about pregnancy? As a commitment?"

"Well, that's extra. That's unplanned, much of the time. It's not really relevant except in its result."

"Which is?"

She stared at me. "The baby. You have a baby."

WHEN I asked my shrink if I was a control freak, he finished saying "Absolutely" before I finished saying "freak." I told him that I once worked with a woman who carried a remote control in her purse. Whenever she got worried or angry, she took it out and stroked it like a gerbil. My shrink said that if I keep comparing myself to severe neurotics, I'll think that anything is permissible.

David, Mona's David, called me up at home. He asked to meet me. I agreed, mostly because I was bored. Adventure, scandal, I told myself. Free drinks. We met in a country-western bar called the Elvis Pelvis.

"Thing is," David said once we sat down, "I know Mona's hiding something from me."

I drank my beer.

"I always considered you a friend, Stephanie," David said.

"Likewise, David." But I didn't. I had only seen him at the occasional barbecue, party, movie. Dinner out, dinner in, hike, rock concert, camping trip, vacation, funeral, softball game. But I was Mona's friend.

Now he touched my hand. "There's nothing I can't handle, Stephanie."

I smiled.

Whenever you spend time with a friend's boyfriend, you grant him a sexiness that he might not deserve, just because your friend finds him somehow desirable. I considered David objectively for the first time. His butt had that expansive thing going on. It wasn't big yet, but just give it a few more years in front of the television. His face was ruddy and childish, but something about his nose suggested that he could have been an artist, that he had a natural, neglected talent for something.

"Who's she fucking?" he asked, which woke me up. I started laughing.

"You're cruel," he said.

"I'm sorry." I straightened my face. "What makes you think something crazy like that?"

"She won't sleep with me. She's had these mysterious disappearances. Overnight. I called and called, and then I went over to her place. She's distant. She's uninterested."

"Maybe she's just . . . uninterested."

"I wouldn't mind that so much. I just don't want to be made an idiot."

I felt sorry for him. I scanned his face, handsome in anger. I was sort of afraid for Mona if he ever found out about the abortion. I realized that I probably knew every single Democrat in Colorado Springs, and David wasn't one of them.

"Why don't you try being supportive of her," I suggested.

"What?" He leaned forward and looked hard at my face.

"Suh. Por. Tive."

"What?" His expression got gentle. "You have something in your teeth."

Horrified, I immediately lodged my fingers in my mouth. "Where?"

"Here." He brushed my hands away and delicately stroked one of my front teeth. I felt the pressure and not the touch. I started to blush.

"There, it's gone," he said. He looked at me again, considering. I tilted my head. I wasn't taken in. But I understood the appeal.

He ruined it by suddenly demanding, "How about a little compassion for me?"

"There is no such thing as compassion," I said. He rolled his eyes, but I'm telling you. Nobody has it easy. Nobody gets anything they don't make themselves.

I VISITED Mona at two o'clock on Saturday afternoon. She opened the door, still in pajamas. She said, "I'm watching a Natalie Wood movie. Wanna?"

The movie was about a pregnant woman who didn't want to get married. Steve McQueen was the irritated father-to-be. She made him drinks and got mad at him, and he played the banjo in the street to make it all better. I didn't really get it. I kept thinking about Natalie Wood falling into the water and never coming up.

When the credits started rolling I asked, "How are you doing?"

"I don't know. I got rid of the fetus because I wanted a life. But now I'm just moping around wondering if I made a mistake. And I've started thinking about God."

"God?"

"Yeah, and Hell. Like, what if it's all true? Let's take a cosmic leap into the possible. What if abortions really do send you to Hell? Then does motherhood make you a saint? Are men just pawns in this game of the afterlife, and women call all the shots?"

"No," I told her, "men murder, rape, declare war. It seems that they have some stake in eternal damnation."

"But abortions seem worse somehow. Because we're impatient. We don't wait to see what happens."

"What would have happened, Mona?"

She shrugged. "I would have been a pissed-off mother who resented her kid. I don't know. Maybe it's like, you're perfect or nearly so in the beginning and little by little your life becomes one long catalogue of mistakes."

"Like bowling," I said.

"So was it fair of me to deprive this fetus of its one shot at perfection?"

"Maybe you did the right thing by sparing it the rest. All those inevitable failures that make us human beings."

"Maybe I should have let all that transpire. Who am I to say, Stephanie? Instead, I killed it. Those possibilities," she amended when she saw my look.

"What about your own possibilities? Did you really want to trade your life for your baby's? Isn't that another kind of murder? Is that what you want?"

"No," Mona said. "But looking at it now, wouldn't it have been a relief? An awful relief?"

I LEFT town to camp alone at the Great Sand Dunes National Monument. As I drove south past Pueblo, the land flattened and rose like acres of brown bread. The high desert. Everything smelled of pinion sap and the things that flow in the desert but nowhere else.

I stopped to look at a roadside memorial. They were scattered all over the roads of southern Colorado, at every sharp corner where someone had perished in a car. This memorial was for an entire dead family—parents and kids. Someone had set up a life-sized nativity scene with gigantic crosses, candles, and silk roses. Strewn about were bandannas, key chains, rosaries, earrings. Plastic flowers in a yogurt container, a Christmas wreath, a macaroni necklace, a wooden cross dangling inside a spaghetti jar, a squash, a stuffed rabbit, a pack of Luckies, a photograph of the mountains, and a scrunchie. For the dead little girl.

I got to the campgrounds after dark. I set up my tent and lay down, but I couldn't sleep at all. I kept wondering if someone would invade my tent with a knife, and imagining what I would do then. I listened to the rustling sounds of other campers, shushing their children or having muffled sex. Finally, I crawled out of my tent, grabbed a bottle of water and headed toward the dunes in the moonlight.

I took off my sandals to wade through the stream that separated the scrub from the sand, and then started hiking the dunes barefoot. At first it felt like I was just pushing sand around with my feet, but then I started moving in the shadows.

I climbed until there was nothing in any direction but hulking masses of sand. I sat on the ridge of a dune, hugged my knees and tried to decipher the shapes. I thought I saw my mother's nose. I saw the shape of a dog I knew when I was small. I stayed there all night, listening to the wind smooth out the surfaces, breathing the smell of sand without ocean, without reason.

In the morning, I opened my eyes to the sun already midway up the sky. I sat up on the dune and brushed sand out of my hair. Everything had changed color now that it was light. Blue sky, yellow sand, and me between the two. I realized that I hadn't been missed. Nobody had noticed me, alone on the dunes or anywhere else. Nobody was going to hurt me; nobody was going to do anything at all to me. I thought about the word *nobody* as I started back toward camp. It was getting hot already. The sand shifted though my sandals. It felt like the tips of matches just barely lit, then blown out.

I MET WITH Mona after I got back from my trip, my skin glowing and rubbed raw. We met at a diner and hugged across the table. She patted her short hair immediately afterwards. "You look gritty," she said. We talked about her work.

After our food came, Mona leaned over her fluorescent grilled cheese sandwich. "We're going to try to get pregnant."

For a second, I thought she meant herself and me. Then, "Oh no, Mona. No."

Mona pulled the paper napkin out of her lap and began shredding it on the table. "I told him everything. He was really hurt. It brought us, um, closer." She turned red while I stared at her. Then she stuck her chin out. "He wants a baby with me. I'm keeping it, this one." She nodded, as if it were merely a matter of will.

"But David? He's ridiculous." I threw my sandwich down on the plate. It made a flat sound.

Mona looked away. "Knock it off, Stephanie."

"You don't even like him that much. You make fun of the

way he *breathes,* for God's sake." I mimicked her impression, this whistling, grunting thing that he does. She does it better.

"He's going to be my husband." The word was designed to stop all debate. I tried one more time.

"But the abortion . . ."

Mona held up her hand at the word. *"Don't* want to think about that. It was a mistake."

"You were so sure at the time."

Neither of us talked for a while. I ate my tired roast beef sandwich, the meat dyeing the mayonnaise pink. Mona played with the napkin scraps on the table. I wiped my mouth over and over, for lack of anything else to do. Mona poked a hole in the crust of her grilled cheese sandwich.

"Mona," I finally said. "You don't even like children. You call them 'yard apes.'"

"Well. I just got . . . so damn lonely, Stephanie. Besides, Jesus." She looked up. "You can't just walk through life like you're a casual observer. I mean, you act like everything is a rational choice all the time, like there's this layer of cellophane between you and the world. You have to engage. *Engage.*"

I snapped, "I am engaged."

"It's human. Everyone needs a family. You can adopt."

"As a single mom? In debt?"

"You have choices. You can find a way to fill in that part of your life."

"My life is good. It's already complete."

But here's what I didn't tell her: compare it to the sand dunes by the full moon, when the absence of light in the shadows is absolute, nonnegotiable. Floating upright and alone on top of the world. The way it feels to walk on such a surface.

WE LOST touch, Mona and I. I missed her wedding with David. The invitation came on a cream-colored piece of cardboard with the words, "It's a Wedding!" embossed on the front. I had to leave town for a business trip that weekend. I sent a gift, something they had registered for—spoons.

Not much changed for me—some dates, a promotion, a new haircut. My grandmother died, I got a dog, and then a cat. The cat hated the dog. The dog liked the cat. That was pretty much my life.

It had been almost two years since I had seen her last when Mona called me at work to invite me to a housewarming party. I scribbled down her new address and said carefully that I'd love to come. Equally carefully, she said that she, David, and their one-year-old baby were looking forward to seeing me.

I drove to her house, a silty number in the worst neighborhood in town. There were bars on the downstairs windows. It was directly in front of a city park where I'd heard you could get a great deal on crack, if you didn't care about quality. There was a liquor store next door, pocked with dirt. In front, a drunk man was talking to a woman in vinyl shorts and red high heels.

When I arrived, the sun had just set behind the mountains. David opened the door, kissed my cheek and led me inside. The walls were covered in cracked green wallpaper, and I said, "How wonderfully retro!" He showed me the garage, which had a workbench and tools all set up on hooks. David looked a little fatter, but healthy and so happy. He couldn't think of anything to ask me besides, "Like my garage?" I laughed, "Yes!" We stared at each other, delighted.

In the center of a group of women, Mona was carrying a big baby in her arms. It drooled on her shirt, and she rubbed at the silk with a cocktail napkin, saying irritably, "Oh, Christ." When she saw me, she smiled and held up the baby like it was an Oscar. We hugged, one-armed. Then she told me the baby's name, which I immediately forgot.

It squirmed in Mona's arms. I leaned down and said,

"Hello." It rattled a fat chew-toy in my face, then rubbed it gently against my cheek. The toy left a viscous smear of saliva and some kind of slime, maybe Gerber's Candied Yams or mucus. The baby announced, "Buh buh buh" above the party babble. Mona said, "Buh buh buh" back, almost sarcastically. Then, "Hold her, will you? I'm starving."

Suddenly, it was in my arms. A real baby. Wiggly. Soft. Yet scratchy.

Mona pushed past her guests and headed toward the kitchen. I wrapped one arm around the baby's sweaty back and cupped its head with my other hand. "Huh," I said, jogging it onto my shoulder.

I remembered something I had read once, that they're supposed to have a soft spot in their skulls, so I started touching its head. Lightly at first, then pressing harder and harder. Nothing, just scalp. It wrapped its tiny hand, which looked like an imitation of a hand, around my hair, which looked real. It started chewing on the hair. I worried about the chemicals in shampoo and conditioner, and the toxins in hair spray. And the smoke from cigarettes, so I walked toward the open sliding glass door, away from the perfume and the microscopic mites that cling to upholstery.

A woman in the party had started to sing "Everything's Coming Up Roses" *a capella*; it was a little performance. Everyone gathered around and someone switched off the stereo. The woman had a voice that was horrible in that trained kind of way. I stared, fascinated. The baby did, too. I felt the baby's body grow taut as it took a deep breath. Then it started to scream.

Mona was somewhere else. Guests looked at us, irritated. I started toward David, but he waved his hand at me—away, away. He mouthed *outside*, and I nodded, just like I was his wife.

I stepped out the sliding glass doors to the shabby backyard. It was long and skinny, running along the house like a moat in front of the shrubs that distinguished the border of the park. I started walking back and forth along the yard in the dusk, my favorite time of day. The baby stopped crying and started pulling my hair again.

The baby was now talking to my hair, calling it buh-buh-buh with an occasional scream. It pushed against my stomach with its feet, and smashed its other hand against my collarbone. The rattle fell from its damp grasp and rolled into the dirt. My left arm was falling asleep. I bent down to grab the rattle, but couldn't manage, so I kicked it out of sight.

That didn't work. The baby was now looking for the rattle, calling to it with vowels of anguish and despair. I tried walking away, but it held out its hands, squirmed and cried. It wanted down. I placed it carefully on the grass near the door, after looking for bugs and broken glass. It stopped crying and crouched on hands and knees, head rigid. Oh boy, I thought.

I hurried across the lawn until I found the rattle, which now looked like a speckled pink egg. I thought of other mothers, and how they cleaned off a baby's pacifier by putting it in their own mouths. I started to put the rattle in my mouth, but just couldn't. Instead, I wiped it on my skirt, where it left a greasy stain.

I turned around to pick up the baby again, but it was gone. Impossible, I thought. I hurried a few steps back to where it had been, but instead of a baby, I saw only a patch of dying grass in the porch light. There was no baby anywhere on the lawn. It was really gone. Gone.

I went back inside to where the party was. One woman looked like she had the baby, but it was another baby. Similar to Mona's baby, but not quite enough. Wearing a purple snuggie, not a green one.

I peered under the tables and chairs. "Did you lose an earring or something?" a woman asked me.

"Uh, no, I lost something else." Nothing between people's feet, in their arms.

"What exactly did you lose?" the woman asked.

It was nowhere in sight—not inside, and not on the lawn. That left only the place where the lawn ended and the park began. It must have crawled that way, toward the crack pipes and heroin needles. I felt sick. I rushed back outside and stepped off the lawn, plunging into the thick brush. My hands trembled as they pulled aside branches. The air grew dimmer.

A twig nearly poked me in the eye, but I swerved in time. I listened hard for baby sounds, then for any sounds at all over my erratic footsteps and the party noise filtering in through the trees. That woman was still singing.

"Baby," I whispered, "oh please."

I began to run, twigs lashing my arms, dead leaves under my feet. I ran in concentric circles. Nobody was there. My feet broke everything I stepped on, snapping dry beneath me. I started to cry. All the colors merged together into varying shades of gray in the twilight. I ran faster.

I nearly stepped on something glowing next to my foot, the shine of tearable flesh. I stopped. That baby was there, sitting perfectly still on a bare patch of ground, eyes open. Yes, the right baby. Not some random baby in the woods.

I bent over and carefully picked her up. We were both shaking. I held her by the armpits and inspected her all over in that raw twilight. I felt her firm, real body beneath her clothes. This little person.

She moved in my hands and looked back at me. Straight in the eyes, just like she was waiting for me to name it. You know. The damage.

Drugs and You

———

He who hesitates is last.

—Mae West

Sometimes he made me tell people how we met, which I hated. He'd make me tell the story in a bar, where you're supposed to be funny, with a punch line. Close to the end, I took him aside and said, "Cliff, our relationship has no punch line," and he said, "Yet." So I told the fucking story, and I'll tell it now that the story's over.

I was new to Santa Fe, looking for a job and friends. I had moved there partly because it was beautiful, and partly because I had lived in Iowa my whole life. Santa Fe had cacti, yet it also had snow. It had a bunch of interesting people who wore silk scarves around their necks during heat waves and hiked in cowboy boots. I wanted to know what made people do things like that. I was almost twenty-five.

It's hard to meet people in Santa Fe because everyone just assumes you're a tourist and doesn't waste time on you. So I mostly took walks alone, or drove around alone, or ate mushy chile rellenos alone in a restaurant called Dave's Not Here. They named it Dave's Not Here because they were sick of people asking for him, Dave. Nobody knows where he is, or, by now, who he is.

One evening in the early fall I was driving down St. Michael's Drive when this man stepped backwards off the median, right in front of my car. I stood on the brakes, but I knew instantly that there was no way, that it was too late. His head turned and our eyes caught through the windshield. My mouth opened. Before the car slammed into his body, he jumped into the air. A football dropped from above and nested itself firmly in his arms before he disappeared.

He was gone. I hit a man, I thought, and sent him to Heaven. I don't believe in Heaven. The car was still skidding forward.

Then the most tremendous thud dented in the car roof, right above my head. I screamed. The car stopped.

Everything was very quiet. I looked up at the roof. I realized that I would have to get out and look at it, the corpse on the roof of my car. I would have to look at the unfamiliar face of a man I had killed. For a second, I wondered how I could die, kill myself, without ever opening the car door.

There was movement above. A sneaker appeared in front. It gingerly reached down the windshield. It snaked around. It jiggled the windshield wiper. Then the whole body slid down onto the hood in a blue blur.

The man was now standing on the ground, feeling his body and neck with one hand. The football was still in the other hand. He looked at it, then dropped it on the pavement. He walked around the car, toward me, and tapped on the window. He asked, "Can you open the window?" He asked, "Are you okay, ma'am?" Then, "Can you answer me?" Other people started running up and pulling out their cell phones.

The man finally opened my door himself. Dust blew into the car and I squinted through it at him. His blue eyes were earnest. "Ma'am? I'm okay. Are you okay?"

I reached for him. He stepped forward to help me. "Ma'am?" I kept reaching past his outstretched arms. My fingers touched the rough fabric of his clothes and I put my hands underneath them, on his skin. I stroked his entire body—his legs, chest, arms, hips, groin, with a kind of wonder at the way a body can just be, or not be. He didn't know what to say. Before I fainted, I touched his face once, twice, three times as if it were the holiest thing I had ever seen.

THAT DAY, after I almost killed Cliff, I wouldn't let him out of my sight. I followed him home. Really, by foot. He kept turning around, saying, "I'm *fine*." After a while, he let me walk with him. He tried to get me to tell him my name, my job, all that. I said, "I'm worried about your head. Don't fall asleep," and he asked, "Ever?"

"Listen, I'm feeling just fine," Cliff said once we walked up to his apartment door. "I just have some bruises on my legs. Don't worry. Let it go."

"I can't. You must be hurt. I hit you with a whole car."

"I have to do some work now." He unlocked his door and stood with his hand on the knob.

"Can I watch you?"

Cliff sighed through his nose.

"I don't really know anyone else in town," I said.

He waved me inside. While he got me a glass of water, I looked around. I noticed the giant photograph of Karl Marx hanging over the kitchen table, and the bumper sticker over his desk: "Jesus, protect me from your followers." His TV was sitting inside a kiva fireplace in the corner. There was a framed photograph of Ho Chi Minh next to a scrawled picture in magic marker of a big green monster wearing an orange sweatshirt. Written above the googly eyes and jagged head was the word "Gog."

"My niece," Cliff said. "I don't know what that means, Gog."

He sat down at his desk. The chair squeaked. I sat on the floor and studied him. He had deep blue eyes and short, light brown hair. Maybe in his early thirties.

"I really have to finish this chapter." He held a piece of paper in his hand.

"What do you do?"

"I'm an economist. I'm working on a book."

"What's it about?"

"The economy. Doom." I guess I didn't have any expression on my face, because he threw his hands up and turned to his desk.

I watched him work. Every now and then he looked up and said, softly, "Please please leave."

So I went home. But I came back.

THIS STORY is about drugs. I'm telling you now because I was surprised, too. But there's more that you need to know.

Cliff thrilled me. He knew words like "anarcho-syndicalism." He *stood* in front of the television set during the evening news and said, "Fuck," whenever scenes of genocide or military strife flashed on the screen. I stared at him. This was real to him. I looked back at the images and tried to stretch my imagination so that it was real for me, too, all the rape and starvation and guns.

Cliff hunted deer every year, up north near Cimarron. He used every part of the dead deer, even tanning the hide himself. He used the deer brain to do it by mashing it up with a bunch of salt. It's called a "brain tan." He told me that every mammal on the planet magically has just enough brains to tan its own hide.

Once we went up to Ojo Caliente to jump in their hot springs. Afterwards, at the package store, Cliff broke out in fluent Spanish. I stared with my mouth open. He and the shopkeeper talked for so long, I just sat in the dust and waited until they were done. The whole ride home, Cliff kept accidentally slipping into Spanish until he stopped talking at all.

In a bar, while Cliff's friends were playing pool one night, he told me that he had grown up in Salt Lake City, as a Mormon. "I grew up believing that when you die, you get your own planet."

"What do you do with it?"

"Whatever you want. You're god."

"Isn't it lonely?"

"You choose your neighbors by marrying them." Cliff raised his eyebrows and nodded.

"Do women get planets?"

"Nope. Sorry. They go to their husband's planet."

Cliff told me that in the Main Temple in Salt Lake City, they have an office ready for Jesus, complete with a desk, separate phone lines, pens and paper. "Mormonism is all about real estate," he said.

"What was it like for you, growing up like that?"

"When you figure out that no deity is keeping tabs on how often you brush your teeth, it's a little depressing. I mean, what's the point?"

"Cavities."

"I mean, to everything? Existence?" Cliff stubbed out his cigarette and lit another. "Nothing. No point."

I grew up with no religion, so I don't have these existential crises, although I respect them in others. I never thought that I was living for the sake of a god. I was just a human being. So it came to be its own point. Life.

WE HAD been dating for months and I couldn't understand why he wouldn't have sex with me. There were many things I didn't understand. Sometimes I lay on his bed while he wrote or read. I rolled onto my side.

"Cliff?"

"Honey?"

"What do you want?"

"Nothing, that's all right, baby."

"What do boys want?"

"Girls."

"That's it?"

"Some boys want other boys."

"What do you want?" I asked. "I mean, what do you *want*?"

"Socialism."

"What do you want?"

And on. Me naked, him reading something, with a cigarette between his teeth.

So I was stupid to have been surprised when I opened the door to his bedroom and found him with a needle in his arm.

We stared at each other for a second. He looked down and pulled the needle out.

"So," I asked clearly, "are you addicted, or just a dick?"

He turned around and opened a desk drawer. He pulled out a bag of needles, razor blades, a scale, a mirror, a bag with a thin layer of white dust, and a small plastic container with a chewing-gum-sized wad of black, sticky stuff. He spread it all on the bed.

I picked up the white bag and cocked my head to one side.

"Cocaine," Cliff said.

I touched the plastic container with one finger. "So, this is heroin."

He opened the container, turned it upside down and then smacked it against the mirror until the wad fell out. I looked at it and its reflection.

"How often do you do this?"

"Once a week. Once a week for three days. Or four. Not so much the rest of the week."

"Why didn't you tell me?"

Cliff touched my face.

I tapped the mirror with the heroin on it. "How much of this stuff does it take to kill you?"

Cliff picked up a razor blade and nicked off a small dab. It was the size of a sunflower seed, smaller, even. I looked at the rest of the heroin lying on the mirror. I had a sudden urge to put the whole gob in my mouth and swallow it.

"Give me some," I said. I was just testing him, to see what he would do, I think.

"No." He put his arm around me. I let him pull me down to the floor and kiss me. It was unreal. I thought about the Mormons and their planets.

I touched that place inside his arms, the small red dot. I was strangely moved by this part of him, so soft, so violated. He kissed me again. Before he closed his eyes, I saw myself curving away in their darkness, and wanted to go to that place where he was.

All that night, I stayed awake and watched over him. He whimpered and reached out for me every now and then. He looked so soft in sleep, fingers curled under his chin. I tried to fit everything together in my head.

I couldn't help it. I know it's very bad. But as I watched him sleep, I felt a strange kind of new respect taking shape. This was a man who sought out a controlled substance and injected himself on a daily basis. Say what you will, but that takes initiative.

I RENTED a movie called *Drugs and You*. We watched it together in Cliff's apartment. It talked about heroin, cocaine, amphetamines, crack, smack, heart attacks, insomniacs . . . I could rap the whole thing. Cliff barely listened. He caressed my hand.

"What you need," he said midway through the rehab stuff, "is a pet. I'm going to buy you a hamster."

"No."

"Everyone needs an animal to love."

"Who says?"

"Nietzsche."

"But I've got you. You're a fucking animal." I gave him a raunchy smile, even though it wasn't true. We barely ever had sex.

"You need something else," Cliff said.

We watched the movie until Cliff got up and disappeared into his room. In a few minutes, I followed him. He was cooking up. This is what my life had become—I knew phrases like "cooking up."

"I can't believe this," I said.

"Why? What did you expect, honey?" He put the needle down. "Listen. This is my life. I don't want to change. On the other hand, I love you. You can do whatever you want with that information."

"Well, tiger, don't get all emotional on me."

He stared at me for a minute. "Once I got so emotional about you, I threw up."

"You threw up over me?"

He brought home a parakeet and named it Fido. He tried to get it to talk, and to sit on our fingers. But whenever Cliff opened the cage door, Fido flew at me, biting. He latched onto my earlobe, or the skin of my neck. He drew blood. I grabbed at Fido and stuffed him back in his cage each time.

"You taste like chicken," I told him through the bars.

Cliff gave up and kept him inside the cage while I was there. I always walked right over to the cage in the corner whenever I came over. Fido and I tried to stare each other down through the bars, his little round eye pitted against my own.

"I might leave you," I told Cliff. But I didn't leave him, and I didn't leave him.

IT WAS OUR anniversary, three months. We were going to go to dinner at La Cocina, and then have sex. We had to plan sex in advance, to make sure that it fell on a sober day—my rules. Mostly because there was no other way to do it.

I showed up at Cliff's apartment but he was late, so I let myself in as usual. I mooned around, in love. I touched things—his calculator, his shirts.

By the time he opened his door, I was already there to greet him. He grabbed me around my waist and held me. I put my arms around him. He said into the air above my head, "I shot up tonight." As his mouth opened to say these words, I felt something drop into my hair. I touched it. It was his gum.

"Oh no, I got gum in your hair. I got . . ." Cliff was distraught, groping the top of my head.

I stepped away and stared at him.

I went into his bathroom and grabbed the edges of the sink. I looked in the mirror. The face that looked back was so ordinary, not the kind of face that can change the world or even the sheets. Cliff soon appeared in the door with a jar of peanut butter.

"I heard that if you put peanut butter on it—" He started painting my hair with peanut butter.

"Forget the hair." I whirled at him. "Forget it." I picked up his nail scissors and cut out the whole wad of hair, gum and peanut butter. I threw it at him.

"I can't live with an addict. I don't want to come home and find you dead in the lotus position."

"We're not living together."

"This is already a very unhealthy relationship," I told him.

He looked slightly relieved.

"I mean, it *was*," I said. "I'm out." I spread my hands wide, fingers stretched open.

Cliff looked down immediately. Then he went to the bedroom. After a second, I followed him. He opened the drawer with all the drugs and paraphernalia. I got suddenly scared, thinking about that little dab of heroin. I started grabbing at his arms, pulling them away from the needles and things. He pushed me away, gathered everything up, and left the room.

I stood in the hallway and listened to the sounds of a toilet flushing, a hammer against metal, plastic bags rustling, then the door slamming. I went back into his bedroom and lay down on his bed, holding my forehead.

I live like a bug, I thought. Crawling around, wondering when I'm going to get squashed. This relationship is a bug.

In a few minutes, he was back in the bedroom before the front door had fallen shut. "You won. It's gone," he said. "All of it."

I sat up.

"Poof," he said.

AT FIRST there was an element of *now what?* In fact, I asked Cliff. "Now what?"

"Well, what did you do with other boyfriends?"

"I don't remember," I said.

But we tried stuff. I read some trashy novels and got ideas. There's always the section of the book after he almost loses her the first time and then gets her back, and they do things during those times. Go to dinner, go dancing. Talk about their family lives. So these were the things that Cliff and I did. We talked about the world. We talked about each other. We saw a counselor who once put her hand on Cliff's knee during a session. We found another counselor and then decided that things were pretty good, so I moved in.

We mixed his books *(War and Strife, Strife and Socialism, Socialism and Revolution)* with mine *(Wuthering Heights, Lolita, National Velvet)*. We took the TV set out of the fireplace and built fires out of pinion branches. We made homemade tamales. We watched Santa Fe's lava sunsets, when the clouds lurk around the east edge of town like ghosts afraid of fire.

But no matter, he shot up again, of course. It was my twenty-sixth birthday. I had just came home from grocery shopping. He didn't tell me. He didn't have to—the way he passed his hand over my face before saying anything, the way his facial expressions appeared one second too late, as if he were following cue cards. I looked up at his face and started to cry.

I wondered how long he'd been doing this. Months? I had long ago stopped checking the insides of his elbows while he slept. Or he could have been smoking it. It didn't matter—it didn't matter. I grabbed his shirt and cried into it, while he just stood there, arms at his sides.

"I don't know how to save you," I said and wiped my nose on his shirt.

"You're not supposed to." He kissed the top of my head over and over.

"But I want to."

"Why?"

Because I want you to save me, I almost said. But I looked into his eyes and realized that there was nothing left to save in either one of us.

A FEW DAYS later, I woke to something rustling around in the living room. I listened again, and there was definitely someone in the living room, picking up papers and putting them down again. I touched Cliff, but he was already awake, staring at the ceiling.

"Somebody's out there," I whispered.

"Yeah," he whispered back. His body was completely relaxed next to mine. He was still high.

"Go out there. See what he's doing," I said.

Cliff's eyelashes beat in the air like the wings of a moth. I dug into his side with my thumbnail.

"No," he said.

"No?"

He turned his head toward me. "No." I could almost taste that word in the dark. No.

A flurry of noise in the next room shot me out of bed. I leaped for the closet, shivering. Cliff's grandfather's old .22 rifle was on the top shelf. I gently lifted it down and unzipped the leather case. The gun was a deep, shining color in the dark, smooth next to my bare skin.

"Is this thing loaded?" I whispered. Cliff made some gesture but I couldn't tell exactly what it was because I didn't have my contacts in my eyes. I fumbled with the chamber, trying to figure it out.

I poked the door open with the barrel of the rifle and stood in the open doorway, gleaming and naked in the dark. "I've got a gun," I whispered. Nothing. Then I took a breath and shouted, "I'm going to shoot you with this gun!"

After about five full seconds of silence, I felt along the wall for the light switch, while trying to balance the gun and keep my finger on the trigger. I flipped on the light and looked wildly around, pupils shrinking.

On the table, amidst the bills and letters crouched a small, black mouse. It sat still for a second, then leaped off the table and raced across the floor. It hopped back on the table again, springboarding from the arm of the chair. I admired it; how agile, how reckless. How noisy. The mouse did a couple of laps around the room and then I lost track of it completely as it blurred and disappeared into the background. Cliff was still in bed, waiting.

Might as well make it worth the wait, I thought. I squeezed my eyes shut, aimed the gun randomly and pulled the trigger.

The gun made a cracking noise and shot backwards in my grip. The butt of the rifle slammed into my upper arm. I felt the blood there rush to fill the shock of the void. I opened my eyes. There, I thought.

Again the house was quiet. Then I heard the rustle of covers stealthily moving across the sheets, and the gentle sound of feet.

At that moment, I thought of my great-grandmother, who had pioneered to Wyoming to be with my grandfather, a man she had met through letters. She thought it was fate, the way they came together across the miles to love each other in a true, true love. She had missed her guess. He was an alcoholic woman-chaser who occasionally beat her with his fist, a whiskey bottle, a whip. Back then, they still promised, "Love, honor, protect, obey." She weighed one hundred pounds.

Once she tried to kill him with a rifle, maybe the same kind as this one. He came home after a night of drunken sex. She waited for him at the door, desperately in love, naked under a gaping fur coat. He saw the rifle in her hands. He stopped short. His hands fluttered at each other. There was the soft click of the trigger. After a second, his shoulders slouched again.

"Aw, Tootie, you'll never be able to kill me," he said and went to bed.

She couldn't figure out what went wrong until she lowered the rifle. The hammer had gotten caught in the fur.

Another night, years later, she looked at my great-grandfather snoring next to her. She slipped out of the bed and threaded a needle in the darkness. Then, starting at his feet, she quietly sewed him tight into the bed covers, using small stitches. It took all night. I have often imagined it, the soft sound of the needle puncturing the cloth with each stitch, the patient click of the thimble against the steel head.

When he was completely stitched up, my great-grandmother put the needle and thread back into the lacquered box and stretched. She slowly pulled on her boots. By that strange light before dawn she trod outside to the shed and found a lead pipe.

By the time she dragged it into the bedroom, he was awake and struggling in the covers. She beat him with the lead pipe until the sun came up.

I wondered if I had what it takes.

Then there was Cliff, haggard in the doorway. I loved him so much. But I saw his slack, withering body. He was slipping. I don't know how I could have ignored it for so long.

He stared at something over my shoulder. I turned around, squinting, with the gun still under my arm. Things had already changed for me before I even saw it, the little black mouse on the table, head blown clean off.

Mercy

———

*I've been things and
done places.*

—Mae West

I found the apartment the day I arrived in New York City. I lived above a Chinese restaurant that served peanut butter and cucumber sandwiches as a lunch special. There was a Room For Rent sign by the cash register. I read the lease over a bowl of rice speckled with anise and crushed coriander. While my pen quivered over the space left for references, Kim, the young landlord asked, "Quiet, right?"

I nodded. A leaf fell from my hair onto the table.

"If I find a cat, it'll be liquidated. Deep sixed. I'll make it into gumbo," he said.

"No cats." I signed the lease. "No noise." *Asshole*, I thought.

Every time I came home, Kim followed me as I wandered among the tables, walked back through the gritty kitchen and started up the stairs to my apartment. "Here, try this," he'd say and I'd pause with my hand on the banister, opening my mouth. He usually popped something in with a toothpick, or if he had no time for a toothpick, with his sesame oil–stained fingers. Sometimes a fresh dumpling but more often an experiment— shrimp *fra diavolo*, or a scoop of shepherd pie. A stuffed jalapeño. Escargot.

I said, "The sign says Chinese Restaurant, Kim. Why do you serve Chateaubriand?"

"My grandfather's French. And we sold four today," he said.

I walked around this city five days a week, too scared to point to a Help Wanted sign and ask, "Really? Really?" I was out of money, and I had never had a job. To leave my husband, I had spent all his cash and maxed out his credit cards. I had felt a kind of pleasure in watching his money slip through my hands until it was gone.

But I did like coming home every day, walking under the neon "Lotus Eaters" sign and up the long steps to my studio apartment, my hot plate, my dishes stacked in the bathroom sink. Sometimes I sat at the one window and watched customers walk into the restaurant. From above, their bodies shortened as they approached until they were just blond, brown or red dots. And then the restaurant door swung open. When I pressed my cheek against the window, I could feel the building shift to make room for one more life, one more hunger.

So many couples, holding hands or arguing. The thought of it now—going out with a man, eating dinner, going home together—seemed no longer possible. Even if I had wanted to, I never would have brought a man home. I can't imagine it—trailing through the restaurant and kitchen, Kim following us with two toothpicks. Watching the man leave in the morning from the window as he grew from a dot to an elongated figure.

So I waited. Waited for the lease to end, waited for a good reason. I was thirty years old then. I told myself, I will wait another thirty before I give up.

A FEW WEEKS after I moved in, I came home from another day of wandering the streets, looking for a job. Kim glanced up from a torn copy of *Jane Eyre* and straightened on his stool. He called, "Moki! Moki!" and hunched his thin shoulders around his ears.

A little boy tottered down the stairs from my apartment, wearing a pair of my underwear on his head. They were purple, out of my dirty laundry pile.

Kim quickly reached out to snatch the underwear from the little boy's head, and then his hand faltered. I grabbed them myself, immediately stuffing them into my coat pocket.

"Where did you get the kid?"

"My son," Kim said. "I just got custody. Long story. I'll spank him."

"Spank yourself," I said. "Why did you let him go into my apartment in the first place?"

"It's not an apartment. It's a room," he said.

I stared. "*My* room."

Furious, I grabbed the kid's balled fist and pried it open. There was nothing inside. Feeling even more foolish, I carried him up the stairs to my apartment. He leaned sideways in my arms and pointed at the cracks in the wall and ceiling. His black hair fanned out like a fish's fin.

Once in my apartment, I wondered what to do with him. So I showed him the window. Then I showed him a bowl. Then I showed him what I was wearing. He sat in the middle of the room, as stoic as a blackjack dealer.

"Talk," I said.

He stared at me with his bluish-black eyes.

"Come on, say something."

"No."

"Where's your mommy?" I asked, cruelly.

Moki pulled at my hand until I sat next to him on the lint-specked floor. Then he grabbed my head and bit my cheek, hard.

I pulled away quickly and touched the milk-tooth indentations with my fingertips.

"That hurts," I told him. "When you do that, you have to do it . . . in your imagination."

"What dat?"

"In your brain."

"What dat?"

Eventually we gravitated into a game of Laundry. The game was this, I guess: I picked him up by his chubby legs until he hung upside-down and his bangs separated from his forehead in staticky lines. Then I said, "Time to do the laundry!" and he laughed and laughed. I set him down carefully on the mattress, head first. Moki said, "Again, Mommy."

"I'm not your mommy," I said. I pulled up my shirt halfway and showed him my stomach.

"See?" I said. "No stretch marks."

He laughed and showed me *his* bellybutton, still an outie. He poked it with a small, perfectly groomed finger, then became lost in its complexities. I looked at the part on the top of his head as he studied.

After a while Moki looked up and said, "Again."

"Again what?"

"Again laundry."

"Laundry's dirty."

"Dirty birdy purty laundry."

I picked him up. He said, "Mommy."

And there we were again.

IT HAD BEEN a month since I had left my husband and taken the first seat on a train headed here. The last words I said to my husband: "Yeah, well, and I hate *Texas*." While he was hitting my face, my hands slid his wallet out of his back pocket.

I called a taxicab from a pay phone outside a convenience store. People stared at me. When the cab came, the driver said, "I don't do hospitals, lady."

I said, "Train." I lay down in the backseat, turned my head and wiped my face against the upholstery.

I don't know how I got up the steps of the train station. At the ticket window, the stationmaster couldn't understand what I was saying, thinking I was drunk or on drugs. I kept pulling money out of my husband's wallet and pushing it through the slot in the window until he gave me a ticket to somewhere. Here. New York City.

I FOUND a job advertised in a flyer and they hired me over the telephone. The job involved telemarketing opera libretti and other junk. On the first day I showed up in my one skirt and my supervisor complimented it. After the third day in the same skirt, he frowned at the stain on my right thigh. He kept glancing at it until I nested a phone book in my lap.

I worked off a typed list of names and phone numbers. The telephone was a dial phone, orange, weighing about fifteen pounds. I started using a pencil to dial, and the fossilized eraser on the tip left green, waxy streaks over the numbers.

It was hard to make a sale, especially when the lists were wrong. "Hello, is Mrs. Morganschleffer available?"

"It's Morganstern. And you have the wrong number."

"Morganstern." But she had already hung up.

Most of them didn't know what a libretto was, which is what I told my supervisor when he complained that my numbers were down. Actually, my numbers were nonexistent. "These phone lists are from carefully selected sources," he scolded. "The opera-listening public."

"Well, they don't seem to know any opera."

"Maybe you should study up on opera so you can tap into the specific selections that they do know."

"When I said 'opera' to one of them, she said, 'I don't watch Oprah. I watch Jerry Springer.'"

"You're not enunciating."

"Can't you give me something that makes better use of my skills?"

"What skills?"

He was right. It was as if I was just born.

My supervisor fired me after he overheard me trying to sell my hot plate and wool coat. He got angry when I said that I was just trying to sell people something they might actually want. "And I'm broke," I explained.

"Survival of the fittest, my dear," he said and slid off his penny loafers to rub his feet in their black ribbed socks. But I didn't know who the fittest would be. He didn't have any other employees. He barely had an office. My desk was a bunch of plastic milk crates lashed together with duct tape. Wood paneling on the walls. Carpet with ridges running down the middle like snake spines.

He paid me in cash for half the week, which was more than I deserved, he said.

After the money was in my hand, I said, "I'm going to think hard of something bad to do to you." He reached to take the money back. I snatched my hand away and then left.

All that evening I sat in the restaurant, watching people, figuring things out. Kim emerged from the kitchen with a hissing *coq flambé* for the table by the door. On the way back, he winked and said, "Kiss me, I'm an Aquarius."

I held Moki in my lap and whispered into his hair, "No money."

He murmured, "No nunny." He patted the stuffed dog I gave him. I had found it in a dumpster and washed it carefully in the bathroom sink with dish soap.

Over his head, I turned a page in the want ads. I circled an ad that said, "Creative energetic person needed for exciting career possibility. Must enjoy dementia population."

Kim hummed as he slapped spatulas and waved towels in the air. Through the open doors, the kitchen swam with char and grease. His hands whirred around a plate until it was dressed with food the way a child is dressed for New Year's. The dangling peels of paint shifted as he walked by, then they settled again.

I watched Kim's reflection through a metal pie case filled with homemade baklava, raspberry torte, and as a concession to Americanized Chinese culture, fortune cookies. Kim made them himself and called them Misfortune Cookies. He stuffed them with handwritten messages saying things like, "Even your Hawaiian shirts can't save you from global warming." I pulled a cookie out of the case and crumpled it open. It said, "You will meet a tall, dark felon."

When Kim pressed his concoctions on me, I always protested. Then I opened my mouth. After the restaurant closed for the night, I sneaked downstairs and stole hamburger and dry bunches of noodles. I heated stained pots of water on his stove. I lay flat on the counter with my cheek pressed against the cold, scrubbed metal. I slipped eggs into the boiling water, and watched to see if they would crack at the shock.

I HAD TO do something. Using Moki's finger paints, I painted a sign that said, "Fortune Telling, Ten Bucks." I sneaked down the stairs, sign faced inward. Kim smiled at me, hands full of plates.

I walked to the park and propped the sign against a park bench, then sat slightly apart from it, as if it belonged to someone else. After five minutes I scooted closer. After another five minutes I moved it and myself out of the park and onto the street. I leaned against a brick wall and waited there until I felt less stupid.

The first person handed me some money and held out his hand. I clasped it by the fingers and looked at the lines. I wondered if this was the right way to do it. His lines were deep, almost as if he had a cartoon hand.

"You are . . . a very passionate lover?" I said.

He nodded. His forehead turned pink so I continued, louder over the sounds of the cars.

"Watch out for airlines with the letter F in them. Less red meat, more fish. Your boss will make a fatal mistake and blame it on you. You will have an affair, but return to your wife."

He smiled and tipped me.

All day, people asked me about the things that were lost to them. Family heirlooms, past lovers, dead children. When they did, I saw language fall away from me like the ties of train tracks sliding beneath me as I moved forward. I held the words tight to my chest and then released them as my grip broke and I let it break.

So it was easy when someone grabbed my hand and asked, "Will I ever see my little Bobby again?"

I said, "Yes, of course."

Or, "No."

KIM ENLISTED my help in the kitchen when a busload of tourists pulled up. I hadn't really cooked in months, so it felt good, the crash of the raw vegetables in oil, the crackling skin of poultry, the moist flakes of fish. Kim said, "Moki, help me. Sing me the song." Moki danced in the hot kitchen with a handful of cabbage. The song had no words, just high noises and the windy sound of his breath.

As I brought hot food to the tables, the tourists said, "Thank you. How lovely." Or, "I never saw cheese in Chinese food before." Then they were silent in their ferocious eating, every now and then glancing at each other with painted eyebrows piled high with emotion.

After everyone had left except for the odd dumpling-eater, Kim said, "And now for us." He pulled a steaming duck from the oven. He showed me how to peel back the fat and baste the surface so it formed a soft second skin.

"So what do you do all day long?" Kim asked.

"I'm kind of a fortune teller."

"What's my fortune?" He held out his hands, stained with grease and black bean sauce.

"Fame." I smiled.

"Do you have a boyfriend?"

"I don't even have a friend."

"What about Moki?" Kim asked. Moki was chewing on the wrong end of a carrot, so I pulled it out of his mouth and turned it around for him.

Kim turned back to the stove. "You're from Oklahoma," he said.

"Texas."

"You talk like a Texan. Can you ride a horse?"

"No."

"What can you do?"

"I don't know."

"I can't do much myself. Besides cooking."

After a few minutes, Kim asked, "Why do you stare like that?"

"I can stare if I want to."

Kim took off his apron, then his shirt. "Look at me," he said, but I was already looking.

He was slightly skinny, with muscles that looked excessive, placed there for decoration only. A narrow rivulet of sweat shone on his hairless sternum. He was a man, clearly. He was a man at a loss.

"Well, what do you think?" he asked, arms stretched out.

Embarrassed, I looked away, and then at his son who was staring at me with a big wooden spoon stuck in his mouth.

THAT NIGHT, Kim knocked on my door, looked at what I was wearing and asked, "Are you ready?"

I looked down. My clothes weren't fantastic, but I was clean. He wore a white shirt and a tie with dice all over it.

We went to a French restaurant. At least, all the names of the dishes were in French. Kim was very interested in what I was going to order, vetoing my first choices with, "Aw, I can make that."

We chatted over dinner. I watched myself just talking like there was nothing else to it. I barely tasted the food, partly because I was used to Kim's cooking by then. Everything else tasted bland by comparison.

Over dessert, I asked, "What happened with Moki's mother?"

Kim leaned over his plate. "When you came here and signed the lease. Were those bruises on your face?"

"Yes," I said.

"I'm sorry," he said.

"That's okay," I said, idiotically.

Kim said, "Moki's mother is in Mexico. She stole some money from her job. She also got very fat. Fatter than you can imagine. She said it was my fault. She was convinced that Moki was a stomach tumor. She called me ugly. She ate hot dogs. She moved out. She cut her hair and then moved out."

"So. You two didn't work out in general. It was a mistake."

"From retrospect, every mistake just looks like denial." Kim folded up his napkin and then just threw it down on the table anyway.

After dinner, we took a walk. It began to sleet. The slush formed a shell over Kim's black hair. He smiled at me. "Look at you. You're encrusted." We grinned at each other and I thought, Spring.

"Am I trying too hard here?" Kim asked.

WHILE I was reading fortunes on the street, a bald man slapped his pregnant wife and drove off in his squad car. The woman steadied herself on the rail of someone else's stoop, then walked slowly down the street, her face still.

She stopped in front of my sign, then sat carefully in the woven folding chair next to it. She started crying into her hands.

"Should I call somebody?" I asked, reaching across the card table but not touching her, not sure where to lay my hands.

"I need something," she said. Her lips receded from her teeth. She held her breath while she cried quietly.

"A doctor?"

She took a long, shaking breath and then several more. Her eyes focused on mine. She asked, "What just happened?"

So I told her that she fell in love with the wrong man. I told her she would have to leave, soon, as soon as she could. I told her about the escape, the ride on the train, the blood and the bruises.

I started to tell her that she would lose this baby in a dirty train bathroom while the tracks blinked fast under her feet. She would think she was dying when she felt the first contraction. She'd feel the bloody mass slip from between her legs and float in the bowl, the baby she didn't even know she had inside her. Tiny. Not more than a few months. She'd realize that it must have just died in her as she walked out on Texas and her husband, with his wallet hidden in her underpants. She would sit inside the bathroom for two hours, staring at the dead baby, until finally she would flush the toilet. From Texas to New York, she would see the tracks constantly renewing themselves in their horrible uniformity, and she'd think that there is no such thing as mercy.

I HAD AN interview at a travel agency. Kim styled my hair for me, and Moki planted a slobbery kiss on my cheek. "Good luck, good luck," they chanted, waving from the window while something smoked on the grill. "Good-bye!"

The agency was eight blocks from home. When I walked in, the women smiled from their desks and batted away cigarette smoke. They were all fat. Scattered on every flat surface were jars of candy, cookies, and packages of snack cakes. A Labrador retriever greeted me, tail flipping around, ears folded like wontons.

"Have a donut," Marjorie, the boss, said. I took one and, without thinking, held it in my lap.

The first question she asked was, "What exactly are your feelings about travel?"

The other women in the office joined in. "Do you know Windows? Oh, it's easy. Hey, how did you get your skin to look so soft?"

"What's that accent, honey? Where are you from?" Marjorie asked.

"Oh, here and there," I said.

They made the dog do tricks. "Maurice—jump! Jump! Well, he usually jumps."

Maurice ran under my outstretched hand, back and forth. "He's a self-petter," Marjorie explained. "Well, you're hired. We can only pay you starvation wages, but there's always food around, so you'll live. OK by you?"

I nodded. Maurice kept moving, trying to milk every last bit of kindness out of what was only a hand, only mine.

After I left, I turned down the first alley I could find. I jumped up and down, hands clenched into fists, grinning. I hopped right by a man lying down along a wall. He rolled over and asked, "Change? Bunny?"

I stopped jumping and reached into my pockets. They were completely empty. I turned them inside out. "I'm sorry," I said breathlessly. "I have absolutely no money." I started hopping again.

"Wait." He reached inside his shoe and then held out something in his grimy fist. I wouldn't come closer until he opened his hand to show me what was inside. "Here," he said. It was a quarter. He tossed it over to me, then rolled over.

*   *   *

MOKI RAN in circles around my room, then picked up my toothbrush, which was lying on the floor for some reason. He started to comb his hair with it, then stopped when I made an Aaa-Aaa-Aaa noise. Then he pretended, lightly brushing a few inches above his head, before then pretending that it was a horse and galloping around the room.

I read a magazine article explaining how to keep a lover interested. This particular article suggested that I call out another man's name in the heat of passion. To keep him guessing.

"Guess what?" Moki asked.

"What?"

"Elephants."

Downstairs, Kim was closing the restaurant for the night. I heard him shut the cash register at the counter. I could picture the way he moved around the place, like a spider—thin enough to wedge in the tight spaces, yet weaving the place together with his long arms. I thought of the way he could flip a fried egg without looking.

The night before, he had made me a special dinner, celebrating my new job. He sat me at the table by the window and plied me with more food than any one person could eat. He made all the customers sing, "For she's a jolly good fellow," conducting with chopsticks while Moki banged a pot with a spatula and marched around.

After the customers left for the night, Kim walked me up to my apartment. He kissed me quickly on the stairs, then slowly. Then he went back downstairs. I just stood there, blushing in the dark, listening to him lock the doors.

Now he walked into my room without knocking and pulled Moki and me off the floor. He led us down into the dim kitchen, where we sat on the counter with the soggy tomatoes and the cucumbers in their buckets.

Kim held my hand in his and rubbed it until it started to hurt. He pushed my hair behind my ears, then held my face in both of his hands. I looked back at his eyes, so dark and definite in shape, like twin teardrops. He let go of my face, and I felt the warmth on my cheeks even after it was gone.

Then he pulled Moki into his lap and said, "It's time for you to tell me everything."

So I told him about Texas.

One night my husband hit me until I couldn't close my mouth. It was stuck open, like I was yawning. Every time I tried to bring my jaws together, something in my temple snapped and I couldn't see very well. I cried like an animal.

He left and the door slammed in a slice of cold air. I waited at the window, in the dark. The dog across the street barked at his chain.

In front of the Our Chance gas station across the street, a faint figure moved under the street lamp. It was an elderly woman, walking, shuttered by passing cars. Her orthopedic shoes had high heels, and something glittered around her neck. Glass beads, probably. Ladies' night out. Her head was doddering back and forth, back and forth.

The cars passed so quickly that it was almost a freeze frame when I first saw the man running behind her, then closer, then raising a fist to strike as the woman peered slowly around her shoulder.

The old woman opened the claw of her fist. I held my breath and grabbed at the surface of the windowpane, but I couldn't see very well. Each passing car obscured her.

She lunged at the man's neck with a karate chop. Her handbag swung from her elbow. She whirled around and jumped. She was up in the air; it was impossible. As she landed, her foot lodged into the man's kidney. He dropped. That was it.

There were no more cars. The man writhed on the ground.

The old woman bent over him, saying something. Her silk dress had a crease in the shoulder where the man had grabbed her briefly, and a rip in the skirt from her—what? It can only be called a flying side-kick. One of her feet lay across the man's throat, as neatly as a table setting.

Then it looked like she'd had enough, because she backed up and then turned around. She adjusted the shoulder strap of her bag and walked away, leaving the man twisted on the ground. Her bun shone behind her, a silver moon.

This is hard for me to say.

I left early the next morning. I took nothing with me besides my husband's wallet and what I wore. Until then, all night, I sat outside on the steps, waiting for him to come home. As I waited, it started to snow. I couldn't remember the last time I had seen snow fall.

The streets grew wet, then hushed with the soft sound of snow on snow. I wrapped my coat around me tighter. I thought about that old woman leaping high and kicking, her old body making new shapes. I had never seen anything like it before. I thought, That could be me. The snowflakes touched my face like a soft reminder. Slowly, so slowly, everything changed from brown to gray to crystal white.

I told myself: This, too, is possible.

Too Big
to Float

———

I generally avoid temptation,
unless I can't resist it.

—Mae West

The first time I flew in an airplane, I ran up to the cockpit, grabbed the pilot by the tie and shouted, "Put it back down!" I was thirteen years old.

The second time, I was flying off to college. I spent the whole time crying, pressing the flight attendant button, and reapplying eye makeup.

The third time, Joe, my common-law husband, gave me fifteen milligrams of Valium and about six of those little airplane bottles of whiskey. I threw up in his lap. We took the train home.

The fourth time was just fine, once we got started. It must have been the crew's maiden voyage. The pilot's voice cracked and shook over the loudspeaker. The flight attendants checked everything twice. They made me pull up my sweater to show them that my seat belt was buckled. As they got more and more nervous, I grew calm. I felt that they understood the full gravity of the situation.

The fifth time was this time. I was flying to Chicago for a memorial service. My stepfather's. He was an ex-pilot. I didn't really know him very well, but my mother did, I guess, and I'm her only blood-child. My stepfather had seven daughters with his ex-wife, when he was a Catholic. Hank and his ex-wife kept shooting for a boy, but failing each time until she was too fat and he was too tired and they divorced each other, saying things like, "Good riddance!" and "Psycho!" My mother said that they became friends later, even bowling together a few times.

At the airport ticket booth I handed the agent my identification. "I want the safest, safest seat on the plane, please."

"That would be the one *inside* the aircraft, ma'am."

"I want to be the only survivor."

The agent frowned at me, and then at my ticket. He said, "Your flight's been canceled. The next one is in four hours and fifty minutes."

Impossible, I thought. I'll never last. "There's nothing sooner?"

He didn't even do that thing where they check their computer and make it all better. "Sorry."

I didn't move. He looked up at me and repeated, "Sorry."

I kept standing there. He said, eyes on his computer screen, "I need for you to move."

I lay my palms flat on the counter. "Listen. I'm scheduled for brain surgery in Chicago at five o'clock this evening."

It worked. With my new ticket, I boarded forty minutes later, telling myself, I can do this. I can *do* this. I can't do this. I quickly scanned the aisles for lucky people: babies, pregnant women, nuns, rabbis, supermodels. I found my seat and strapped in so tightly, I felt nauseous. During takeoff, I busied myself by scrabbling in my bag for the little Valium pills Joe had given me, but they were lost or crushed somewhere in the folds.

At the first bump, I gripped both armrests, knocking someone's arm off. I turned to apologize to the woman next to me. She said, "Don't worry, 90 percent of plane crashes happen when the plane is taking off or landing, so we're halfway safe."

I snapped, "*All* plane crashes happen when the plane is landing. That's what a crash is. Landing, hard."

She was still kind, pulling the plastic window shutter down, which just made it worse because then I had no frame of reference at all.

Drinks were canceled because of the turbulence. I kept reaching for the airsick bag and then pulling my hand back, as if it were an exercise. The woman next to me followed every motion out of the corner of her eye. The plane lurched around the sky. I thought, we're getting derailed somehow. I told myself, it's a plane, there's no track. It's a plane, it's too big to float in *air*.

Just then, I felt a stunning blow to my head and everything turned fuzzy for a minute, then crooked. A flight attendant shot up next to me and asked, "Are you okay? Ma'am?"

I looked down at the new object in my lap. It was a computer case. A computer had burst out of the overhead compartment and landed on my head.

"How many fingers?" the flight attendant asked me. I just stared at her. "How many am I holding up?" She waved her hand in my face. I opened my mouth and waited for some sound to come out.

"Don't you know?" I finally asked. "They're your fingers."

She left to get me some ice, while I tried to focus my eyes. I turned around in my seat and looked at the people behind me, sleeping with their mouths open, jiggling in their seats, heads tucked into pillows or leaning against briefcases. They all seemed so fragile. I wanted to open my arms to all of them and gather them up, these bags of souring flesh and veins. I would ask them, is there a safe place somewhere? Where we can go? Can we go there now?

I CALLED my mother when I got to my hotel room. She was making potato salad for the post-service reception the next day. She was frying bacon. "It has to be German potato salad, because, well, Hank was German." Her voice wobbled a little.

"Oh, Lois. He always was a fascist about such things." Then she cried openly for a while, as I murmured on the other end, and tried to match the uneven strips of hotel wallpaper in my mind. When I asked if I could come over, she said, *"No."* She was too busy to entertain, she said.

I wandered into the hotel lounge for a drink. In Chicago, everything's built out of this beautiful cherry-stained wood. You'd think they would have learned after their big fire. Their big cow-fire. Maybe they felt lucky in the way that survivors do, figuring that disaster couldn't strike twice.

The pilot from my flight was there, at the bar. His hat was off, but he hadn't changed out of his white polyester suit and dumb red tie. It had to be the same person—how many pilots have red hair? He was slurping a margarita with salt daubed all over the rim. I glared at him and slid into my own booth. He smiled, unable to tell the difference between flirting and rage.

The pilot sent over a drink. I didn't even glance to see what it was before I shot out of the booth and walked up to him. He flashed his teeth at me. I said, "I should slap you in the face."

The smile vanished, then reappeared. "Oh?"

Not even a proper question. "You flew like shit. I thought we were going to die. A computer fell on my head."

"Well, that explains it." He turned back to his drink. I sort of stood there for a minute, then walked away to my own table.

I'm not too lucky with men. Joe and I had, after three years of living together, settled on a place of total misunderstanding. We had different views about everything, from metaphysics to pizza. Joe said that fun is the goal of life, but I disagree—I think having a goal is the goal of life. When I said that, Joe said, "Say 'goal' more than twice in a sentence and it becomes gibberish." Then he said, "goal goal goal goal goal goal" until I covered his mouth.

Now, at my table in the hotel lounge, I said aloud, "It's better than not having a goal at all." Joe thought his job was very complicated and soul-satisfying. He was a short-order cook. Miles away, in Chicago, I said, "Hah!" The pilot turned around to look at me and I pretended to be doing something important with my napkin.

I have this habit of talking to my boyfriends past and present when they're not around. The odd comment, like, "You always hated my hair anyway," on my way to the hairdresser's. Or, "But what about that checkout girl you slept with?" at the pivotal point in a movie when the woman takes the man back. And there was no checkout girl, in the movie or anywhere else, really.

I realize that this is what crazy people do, while doddering down the street with their grocery cart of shoes and empty Woolite bottles. But I'm not crazy. Maybe nobody's crazy, maybe they're just . . . startled, all those talkers-aloud, those women with tight cigarette clouds above their heads, the ones who slap their hands flat on the table and shout to nobody in particular, "But Nixon *was* a crook!" Maybe it's just a combination of feeling too much and too little at the same time. Maybe they're hoping that someone, anyone will say, "Yes, he was. That bastard."

THE MEMORIAL service was the next morning at ten o'clock, in a church in Lincoln Park. The church wasn't far from the hotel, but I walked for blocks down the shaded streets before I found it. It was pretty warm for springtime, and I was sweating. I was wearing the only black dress I owned, which was, unfortunately, vinyl. If there had been more time, I would have shopped.

Before the memorial service, Hank's seven daughters all clustered together. My mother greeted me and I said, "Hi, Mom!" in a big voice. The seven sisters glared at me and I remembered that a funeral is the only time when you're not supposed to be glad to see each other. My mother's shoes (forest green) didn't match her dress (navy blue). I guessed that she had dressed early in the morning, when the colors all look the same. She looked at me like she could place my face, but not my name.

During the service, I tried to cry, but I had only met Hank a handful of times. Each time he had given me a stick of gum. People stood up during the "sharing" portion of the memorial service and every single one of them said, "a great guy." Tears leaked out of my mother's eyes the whole time. That almost made me cry, but even that didn't work. Having escaped death myself on that plane ride, I didn't feel much sympathy. Heart attack, yes, I know. But I was ready to believe that it was his fault, somehow. After all, he was the one with the heart.

The reception was in the church cafeteria—fluorescent lighting and linoleum floors. I ate prodigious amounts of potato salad, while the real family stood and talked to people. Hank had been right—it *was* good. Nobody talked to me. I looked around at the crowd. Even the old biddies looked stylish, all in black. I softly sang a song I vaguely remembered from somewhere, *"You wore black and I wore black, you wore black and I wore black . . ."*

Someone tapped me on the shoulder, and I turned around, ready to look consoling. Finally, I thought, I get to do what I came here for. But it was some strange man that I didn't know.

"Excuse me," he said. "I just wanted to apologize for yesterday. I didn't know you were bereaved."

He wore black *(and I wore black)*, so I didn't recognize him at first, out of uniform. And then I sucked in my breath. "You," I said. Herr Pilot.

He thrust a cup of punch into my hand, adding something from a flask. "Hank was my flight instructor when I was a kid."

The drink was sweet, mixed with the acrid, pine cone taste

of gin. I remembered that Hank had been a pilot. Maybe that was the reason for all the gum.

The pilot said, "You know, there's this thing called weather. It sometimes makes flying difficult. And turbulence is the least of it."

"I'm afraid of flying, anyway." I admitted. "I'm thinking of taking the train back."

"To where?"

"Seattle."

"From Chicago? It's so inconvenient."

"So is dying," I said, and gestured toward the swarms of gussied-up people in the cafeteria.

He nodded. "I used to be afraid, but not like that. I've seen cases like you. Once, this man locked himself in the bathroom and wouldn't come out, even after we landed. Another man tried to open the emergency exits. One guy prayed loudly the whole time, and kept unbuckling his seat belt during turbulence to kneel in the aisle. And this one woman, upon disembarking, hit me over the head with her purse." The pilot ate a cookie, laughing through his nose so he didn't blow crumbs everywhere.

I liked him. He was very good-looking. I could already guess how this was going to go. It starts out, I hate him, he hates me. Then we discover our common bond—death. We fall in love and have children. Then I get all *Feminine Mystique*-ish and unhappy and he stays out late and I'm stuck baby-sitting, which I don't mind because I'd rather watch Pokémon videos and play with an Etch-a-Sketch than talk to my husband, who's sleeping with a stewardess anyway. Then—what? We get counseling? Divorce? Do we risk it, or do we just walk away?

"Do we risk it, or just walk away?" I asked him, to see what he would say.

He ran his hand through his red hair. "Sure." He took my arm.

"Sure what?" I took it back.

He crumpled his empty plastic cup in his hand and tossed it into the open garbage can, a perfect shot. "Let's blow this place."

OF COURSE, I told him that I couldn't just bag my mother's husband's memorial service, so I said I'd meet him afterwards at the hotel for a drink.

I stuck around and tried to be within reach of my mother. My mother always liked me to be close by, but not too close. When I would lift my arms to be hugged as a child, she'd push me away, saying, "Lois, it's too hot," or "It's too cold," or "Go brush your hair." On the other hand, I found this strappy harness thing in my box of old baby dresses. "What's this?" I asked her.

"Oh, that was your leash. When you were a toddler," she said.

"You put me on a leash?"

"You kept getting lost in the supermarket."

My father had gotten lost, forever. I grew up believing that he was in Jamaica with his new wife and son—when I got older, my mother laughed. "Jamaica *Plain*," she explained. "In Massachusetts." But I still think of him as a Jamaican man, maybe black with long dreadlocks and a smooth, vowel-laden accent. Although, as my mother pointed out, pinching my white skin, this is impossible.

My mother now grabbed me and pushed me down into a chair. "Lois. There's something I want to tell you, right now, while I'm thinking clearly." She slurred her words. I thought, *stroke.*

"Mom?"

"Love isn't the most important thing. Don't lose yourself to it. Lose . . . only a little bit. Because men die first."

"Yes, Mom."

"And you can't lose everything."

"Yes, Mom." I realized that she was drunk. "Mom?"

"Honey?"

"What are you going to do now? After I leave?"

She looked like she was considering this thought for the first time. Then she put her grizzled head down on the table and started crying. Her back quaked under my hand. I patted it until the seven sisters swooped down and gently led her away from me.

I called Joe from the pay phone in the church basement. I stared at the spackled ceiling as he told me that our cat had thrown up on the carpet.

"Joe, what would you do if I died?"

"I'd be *sad*."

I waited, but that was all he had to say. "That's it?"

"What do you want from me, Lois? Don't get all melodramatic. You barely knew the guy."

After I hung up, I kicked at a snag in the carpet for a few seconds. Then I tried to think of Joe's good qualities. He was generally kind. He was generally clean. He had fantastic abdominal muscles. He knew how to pronounce "rhetoric" and "Goethe." He would be there when I came back. I remembered this one time when I was little, my aunt leaning over the coffee table toward my mother, saying that she only wanted one thing: a man that comes home. Joe comes home.

The pilot was waiting for me in the hotel lounge when I walked through the door. The dark was soothing. I collapsed into the booth and lolled my head against the leather. I looked at his face. It was kind and handsome, with a strong chin and dark, smoky eyes.

"What's your name, anyway?" I asked.

"Max."

"Max, I'm married."

"Oh." Max frowned.

"Common-law married."

"Oh." He brightened up. Then, "Do you love him?"

Joe and I had been in love, but it had never felt like true love.

It felt more like true war. There were battles, there were sides. Negotiations, strategies, donuts. Sometimes we looked at each other and secretly thought, *why*?

Max said, "With my ex-wife, it was the same thing. The relationship reminded me of this bumper sticker I once saw on the back of an old Ford Pinto. It said, 'Hit me and we all die.'"

"With Joe, it's like emotional strip poker. I feel like I'm always saying, 'okay, so I don't need my pride. I don't need passion. I don't need commitment.'"

Max told me about his crime-fraught youth. "Once, my friends and I were arrested for frolicking in a fountain. I spent the longest night of my life in jail. I was in a cell between two drunks who were trying to organize throwing a roll of toilet paper from one cell to the other. All night, one drunk asked over and over, 'Did ya get it?' And then the other would ask, 'Did ya throw it?'"

Max had become a pilot because he was afraid of flying. "I was like you, but Hank helped me manage my fear. Sometimes the fear is what makes it so spectacular."

"I'm terrified of falling."

"But that's the best part. So much of flying is falling, anyway. Watch a bird, sometime. And it's so incredible up there. The clouds . . ." He made a helpless gesture. "I can't explain it."

But I knew what he meant. When you fly through a cloud, it becomes just white, glaring light. And if you started falling right then, you would never know it, because you feel like you're falling anyway, not floating, just falling through the air, like a wish.

WE ATE AN early dinner at a hot dog place called "Top Ten Hot Dogs." "What does that mean, Top Ten Hot Dogs?" I asked, mouth full.

"I don't know." He had a plate of different hot dogs, a hot dog sampler.

We rated our hot dogs—I said that mine was definitely in the Top Ten, lifetime, but Max said he thought one of his was maybe number eleven.

"When you get scared, what do you think about?" Max asked. "In an airplane, I mean."

"Dismemberment. Decapitation." I had seen this TV show about a neuroscientist in medieval times who was going to be decapitated. He asked his friend to count the blinks of his eyes before he died, after his head was cut off. He blinked thirteen times. They have since deduced that it takes about ten post-decapitation seconds before you lose consciousness.

"I'm just thinking of that friend, standing over his severed head, counting," I said. "To thirteen."

"How inhuman. I could never do that. Could you?"

"Of course not," I said. "God. Huh! Geez." But I wasn't sure. "If I could, would that make me a sociopath, or a scientist?"

"Scientist." Max touched my face. "Definitely."

I instinctively tilted up my chin to feel his touch lingering along my jaw, then I realized what I was doing and looked down, quickly. "It's the ten seconds that scares me. I'd rather not know when I lose my life, or my mind. What's the name of that brain disease?" I asked.

He swallowed the last of his hot dog. "Which one? The one you have, or the one I have?"

"Kuru. Cannibals get it. You eat people, and your brain turns into Swiss cheese, but you're happy. I want that."

"You want that? Okayyyy . . ." He slowly slid the tab over to me. "Sociopath."

"Scientist." I pushed it back to his side of the table.

"Hanging out with you is like rubbernecking at an accident scene," he said, pulling out his wallet.

Max's first love was a woman named Anita, in first grade.

Max was a dirty, scrappy kid, and Anita was a prissy little thing, always in bows. They played together every day at recess. Once the teacher caught them in a lovers' quarrel. Max didn't remember the story, but his mother told it many times, at parties. Apparently, the teacher sat them down and told them to describe their feelings. She pressed Max to go first. He wiped the dirt off his face, and Anita smoothed down her pretty little skirt. Max took a deep breath and said, "I don't appreciate it when you call me butt-fungus."

Max now said, "Even then, I liked girls with an edge."

My first love was Dean Russo, in the third grade. I was eight when I fell in love with him. It happened like this:

We were lined up in the hall, waiting for art class. The boys were against one wall, the girls against the other. In between was the DMZ. No conversations crossed the hall—any words to boys would have suspended in the air and spelled themselves out in big cartoon letters for everyone to laugh at. The boys punched each other and pretended we didn't exist. We did the same, minus the punching.

When Dean called my name, everyone looked up and stopped talking. So it was in perfect silence that Dean said, "Lois, I like you. A lot."

There was an audible collective breath. Then the whole class shouted mockery about kissing and underpants.

Through all this, Dean still looked at nobody else but me. His eyes were perfectly round, like the blue M & Ms that hadn't been invented yet, like twin planets, like an eight-year-old's eyes when he hasn't yet learned what anyone has to lose.

IT WAS NIGHT, and we were drunk. We had wandered from the hot dog place to a restaurant for cheesecake, then to a gay bar called "Manhole," to a nongay bar named . . . I don't know. We ended up at the pier. Max held my elbow to steer me around a woman who had abruptly bent over to tie her shoe. The lake water made little sucking sounds against the dock. We watched the lights of the Ferris wheel. Max reached for my hand. We held hands all along the pier, and it felt foreign, but good. Then he kissed me for a long time, next to a man in a clown suit blowing up balloon animals.

Max gently propelled me forward and we walked away from the pier, toward wherever we had parked. Two consecutive streetlights flickered on just as we passed below them. We watched other couples jiggling their leftovers, the greasy, white skins of the Styrofoam boxes shining under the lights. A telephone rang inside someone's dark apartment.

When we reached Max's rental car, a parking ticket flipped around under his windshield wiper. Max went through the Five Stages of Grief right there on the sidewalk: "No! Fifty dollars? I don't believe it. Those fuckers! This pisses me off. Maybe I can strike a deal; maybe I can . . . How depressing. I'm so bummed out. Oh well." He smiled at me. "It was worth it."

I fell—bam! —in love.

"This sucks," I said. He nodded, still looking at the parking ticket.

I FULLY intended to stay faithful to Joe. But we barely made it inside the elevator before we collapsed into each other, making out. We rushed into Max's hotel room and slammed the door. And then, just . . . something happened. That something was probably him putting his hand down my pants. Even so, big passion. I had never felt anything like it before. We frantically groped each other. I unbuttoned his shirt. He pulled at my bra strap. I felt like we were going to eat each other alive. "We'll get kuru," I mumbled, and he laughed, and then we got serious.

I thought of Joe, who would be waiting for me tomorrow at the airport, food still under his fingernails. His smug face

floated into my brain. Then I pushed it away, thinking, *Toto,
we're not in Kansas anymore. Tomorrow, we'll go back there.
Right now, we're in a tornado.*

Afterward, I drifted my fingers over Max's chest and said,
"The earth *moved*, baby."

Max said, "I could get serious about you." He dug his nose
into my sternum.

"Seriously?"

We ordered from room service, even though we weren't hungry, and then just picked at the French fries and poached eggs.
We devoured the pie. I felt at home in his hotel room, just like
mine, with the same Al Capone-ish wallpaper and furniture. I
automatically looked for bullet holes.

Then Max sat up on one elbow. His chest hair was curly and
red with some gray mixed in, soft against my hand. He said,
earnestly, "Go to Aruba with me. I'm flying there tomorrow. It'll
be free. You can sit in the cockpit and see how it's all done. Once
you know, you won't be so scared anymore."

I laughed, watching the blades of the ceiling fan drift around
and around.

"Come away with me," he said. "We'll get tans. We'll drink
drinks with little umbrellas in them."

"Really? Umbrellas? Promise?"

"They open *and* close."

"What else?"

"We'll buy matching hot-pink bathing suits."

I was drifting off. "Bikini or one-piece?"

He stroked my face and arms. "Whichever one you want."

"I want everything," I murmured and fell asleep.

IN THE MORNING, Max was all sleepy and soft. We both had
wicked hangovers. He kissed me before he even brushed his
teeth. He also let me borrow his rental car so I could drop by my

mother's, and I rushed out without showering to say good-bye to her.

I found her place in Lincoln Park, in a row of houses all connected to each other. She buzzed me in, and I walked through the dim hallways, looking for her.

I wanted the encounter to be quick and painless, but she was sitting on the hard tile bathroom floor. The faucet was running. I turned it off. My mother was holding up a sock—a cheap, white gym sock with stripes on it, for a man.

"I don't know whether to wash it or throw it away," she said. "Or to leave it like this. Or what."

"Mom, let me stay and help you with all this stuff." Hank had been a pack rat, and decades of junk was tucked away, all over the house. We wandered through the narrow hallways, looking at the swizzle sticks, golf tees, bandannas. A big, blue urn. I picked it up and held it, looking at the designs on the side. I admired its heft, its solidity.

My mother pointed at it. "That's Hank."

I looked down at the urn, then inside. There were ashes in a plastic bag. Hank's. My mother watched as I reached inside the urn, and then inside the plastic bag. I pulled some out. Hank's ashes didn't look like what I expected them to look like. I was thinking of black newspaper ashes, but these were almost flesh-colored, powdery, with bits of bone. Bits of Hank bone. My mother watched me, and I realized that she was watching me learn about ash.

"Do you ever stop being a mother?" I asked her.

"No."

I was still holding a handful of ashes. "Do you ever stop being a wife?"

She picked a piece of bone from the ashes in my hand, studying it. Then she closed her fingers around it and pressed it to her cheek.

*   *   *

MY MOTHER sent me away with a hard kiss, saying that she wanted to be alone. I begged her to let me stay, but she waved me away. "Go home," she said.

I picked Max up and drove him and our bags to the airport. On the way, he talked about Aruba and the beaches, and the water. I kept thinking about my mother, sitting on the bathroom floor, water pouring out of the faucet.

Max led me into the airport, talked to some airline people to get me tickets, and pulled me down the passageway to the plane. He marched right onto the thing, but I balked at the entrance, standing there with my hand on my hip. Max turned around slowly.

"No," I said.

"Lois, more people are killed each year by donkeys than die in plane crashes."

"More people are killed each year by squirrels than by sharks," I offered, stalling.

"The average human eats 3.5 spiders per year." Max wiped his forehead, trying to stay in the game. He looked tired.

"How?"

"They crawl in your mouth while you're sleeping."

"Gross."

"Lois," he said, and I noticed how my name sort of rhymes with "gross." "Get on the plane. Get your hand off your hip."

I shifted.

He said, "Aruba. Aruuuuuuba."

He said, "I know how to drive these plane things, you know. I read a book about it once. You just point and shoot."

He said, "C'mon. Hand. Off. Hip. Move."

But I couldn't. Didn't.

He waited as I looked at him in his uniform, all the way over there, in the plane. He was gorgeous, gorgeous in that way a person is when you've seen him naked, but only once. I wanted to reach out to him, but just then a stewardess appeared, welcoming me to the friendly skies. I looked at her and at Max, wondering if he had fucked her or would fuck her eventually or someone like her, and what was wrong with me in general.

Max looked away and said, "I can't believe this." His face grew rigid with pride. He said, "You're afraid of everything!"

"You don't understand. I don't think I can do it, Max."

"Will you do it for me?"

I didn't say anything. I was thinking.

"Do it for me." His hands were curled into fists on his hips.

I tentatively moved one foot forward, onto the plane. Well, I did it in my head. I meant to do it. Before I got the chance, Max whispered, "Coward," with what looked like tears in his eyes. He readjusted his cap and stormed into the cockpit. I stood there for a minute. "Coward?" I asked. The stewardess was still smiling. "Coward?" But it was true.

Back at the gate, I sat in one of the plastic seats, wondering if he would come back out. I thought about the way he had looked at me in bed. I thought about his warm body underneath his uniform, and how he had felt last night under my hands. How it was possible that I could really love this man. And I wondered what it would take to get me on that plane.

An hour later, the airplane ground away toward the runway, this monstrosity with my pilot on it. It lined up to go, and then built up speed, heading for oblivion. I didn't cry, I didn't wave. I just watched the plane through the airport window as it blew up in the sky, bursting into flames and falling to the earth in chunks of twisted metal and flesh.

No, it didn't.

Instead, it shot away into the sky like a bullet just missing its target, the heart.

Other People's

Mothers

———

"So, you're Ruby Carter."

*"The only thing my mother
ever told me. Everything
else, I found out for myself."*

—Mae West

While Wanda had an abortion, I had lunch with her mother. "Please," Wanda said, swathed in large paper napkins, "just get her away from here." Then she closed her eyes and her boyfriend Ramon nodded, so I took Wanda's mother to a Chinese dumpling shop.

Once there, she told me the old story about how Wanda's father wanted to name her *Espinaca*. Spinach, in Spanish. How Wanda was a fragile child, so delicate that she once cut her finger on a bread crust.

She kept mispronouncing Wanda's boyfriend's name and dropping dumplings. Finally she stabbed a dumpling through the middle with one chopstick and used the other chopstick to saw it in half. "I just love other cultures," she said, "but this is ridiculous."

Wanda's mother: long, gray hair in a single braid, with cheekbones that shot her face forward. Wearing a purple smock with orange trim and tapping her bitten fingernails on the table—"Do you think they're done? Oh my. Oh my shit."

I said, "It's going to be okay, Nancy," or some stupid thing. She stared at me.

"This is my granddaughter or grandson, theoretically. Although a fetus isn't yet a human being. And a woman has a right to choose. But someone's vacuuming out my daughter's insides. Since she came from my insides, et cetera, things aren't as separate as you think, missy. And let me tell you, if it had been legal in my time, I would have done the exact same thing with Wanda." Wanda's mother straightened her smock.

"So do you have regrets now? With Wanda?"

"There's always regret after you act, or don't act. That's true of any big decision."

She was so imperious with her garish clothes and outdated perfume, I said, "Will you be *my* mommy?" She laughed. Then she stopped laughing with a frown and put her hand on her stomach.

When I came back to the clinic, Wanda asked, "How is she?" She was hooking her bra and pulling her sweatshirt over her head.

"Fine," I said. "Stoically liberal."

"Where is she?"

"Getting sick in the bathroom."

We waited at the ladies' room door for Wanda's mother until she reemerged, smiling at Wanda with watery eyes and arms stretched out. "My baby," Wanda's mother said then halted, knowing she had said the wrong thing.

Me, I lost my own mother, although she's still alive. Some nights in my apartment I light a fifty-cent glass candle with a picture of St. Jude painted on one side. I recite the prayer pasted on the back—*Oración a San Judas Tadeo*—knowing little Spanish, besides *espinaca* and some swear words. *"Glorioso apóstol, San Judas siervo fiel,"* I say, "bring my mother back to me," but the painted face says, There are other mothers.

I DATED Macon for two years because his mother took my arm when I met her and said, "Make sure he eats broccoli, OK?"

For me, more than a mother. She was my second-chance mama. I loved her, hemmed my pants for her. I followed her around her apartment, asking questions: "How do you knit? What are basted eggs?"

Macon's mother prefaced her sentences with, "Guess what?" She told guests that I was her third daughter, which caused confusion when Macon and I held hands and kissed.

I learned the rules—what to cook for holidays, what to say about the movies we saw together. If there was a dog in the movie, it was a good movie. If there were guns in the movie, it was a good movie.

Macon's mother thought I needed "toning down" so she gave me a book entitled *Wherever You Go, There You Are.*

"You run around too much. You need to *smell those roses.*" With each word, she pounded the cutting board with her sharp fist.

"It's hard to manage my time. A girl's got to make a living," I told her, dicing garlic.

"It's just as easy to fall in love with a rich man as it is to fall in love with a poor one. Marilyn Monroe said so, and look how well she turned out."

I stared.

She amended, "Well, before that overdose business. Anyway," pointing the turkey baster at me, "*you* need a rich one."

"But what about Macon?" I asked her. Her son. In the next room, his balding head shone in the lamplight. He pulled a hair out of his mouth, then looked at it.

"Oh," she said, "Well, there is that."

She called the day I broke up with Macon. I cried so hard, the phone kept slipping from my hand.

"I'm just so shocked," she said.

I mumbled something that had no words.

"Lunch," she promised. At her house. I'm still waiting to be fed.

*   *   *

WHEN I WAS small, my mother told me the things that a mother tells little girls in order to get along. She told me that when you drink something hot, never sip it the first time. Instead, dip your top lip into the cup. That way it looks like you're drinking, but instead you're testing.

"What if you burn your lip?" I asked.

"It's not as bad as a tongue."

So I did, burned my lip with the milk-laced tea, it was too hot. I thought of what would hurt least—an elbow, an earlobe. Nowadays I poke my finger in the cup, even in restaurants, on dates.

My mother told me, "No, serial killers are not people who kill cereal. No, numbers have no smell. No, dead bugs don't dream."

She arranged concentric circles of bite-sized dabs of cream cheese in a pastel plastic bowl. I scooped them up with my fingers and poked them into my mouth. She picked my grapes off their spines. She pretended that my sandwich could talk, flapping its bready lips. "Eat me," it growled in her hands.

My mother sang "You Are My Sunshine," skipping over the part about waking up and finding your sunshine gone. She pulled warm clothes out of the dryer and dropped them on top of me at naptime.

She said, "There are two to eight calories in each and every stamp."

She did mother things.

She told me that rivers come from rain.

NEXT WAS Frederick. His mother had grown up poor in the Depression. She often quizzed me:

"Do you ever leave the knife in the peanut butter jar and just close it up tight like this?" She screwed the top on. The knife clunked thickly inside. When I said "No, never," she put the jar back on the shelf. "Saves," she said, nodding her head.

"Do you ever leave the cheese cutter in the bag with the cheese? Saves."

"Do you ever put the cooking pot in the refrigerator with the food still in it? Saves."

She told me about sewing across the toes of her old torn socks and putting them on her kids' feet so they'd be warm walking to school, with socks that ran all the way up their legs.

During her entire weeklong visit, she insisted on staying in our one-bedroom apartment. She said, "Oh, just throw me in the corner with a chocolate bar and I'm happy as two clams." We gave her our bed and slept on the floor ourselves. In the morning she said that the mattress was a bit hard, which it was.

She said, "There are three ways of telling time: where you lived, where you worked, and whom you went out with. It's a good idea to keep these things written down on a piece of paper."

When I lived with Frederick, I loved him with a subtle desperation that was tied to anticipated loss. I watched my diet, eating whole grains. I washed everything twice. I put pennies in a jar, skimped on tips. When he finally did leave me, I felt dazed and relieved. As if my grip had grown so tight, only after it was broken could I again move my hands.

Frederick's mother didn't call me. She was on a singles cruise at the time of the breakup, and she probably forgot after that point.

Frederick wrote his good-bye note on the back of our electric bill, which was in his name. I tore it up with the tips of my fingers and flushed it down the toilet, a silly smile on my face. "Saves," I said.

WHEN I WAS about six, my mother had begun sleeping all the time.

She took a nap right after making my stepfather's tepid

breakfast and sacking any lunches for the day. The kiss at the door, then she moved toward the couch as if she was walking down the middle of a canoe. Once outside, I watched her through the tinted front windows of the house. Every morning she fell backward onto the couch, picked up her book, laid it like a tent on her pink terrycloth chest, and closed her eyes. Then I ran off to the waiting bus at the bus stop.

My teacher showed us the parts of a peanut. She told the girls, you can be firemen, or mailmen. Or policemen. I thought about my stepfather's fists when my mother typed up her resumé, and my mother's bruised face the next morning.

After school I always rushed home to tell my mother all the new ways I had learned that she was wrong. She was usually awake when I came home, with her cheek creased from the seams of the upholstered couch pillow. She poured orange juice and pulled out the peanut butter jar. Then she left me an open-faced sandwich with the spoon still stuck in the middle as she went to lie down.

At night, after my stepfather hung up his pants and my mother toppled back to the sofa, I went upstairs to my room, there being no other place. Hoping my mother wouldn't wake up as my stepfather locked my bedroom door behind him, saying, "You like this," as I said, "Okay."

When I finally told her, she kicked him out. After a couple of years.

"You ruined my marriage," she told me.

When my friend Wanda was eleven, she was walking down the street with her mother. Six or seven teenage boys started hooting from a fire escape railing. "Hey baby, hey mama," things like that. Wanda's mother stopped in the street, confused. Encouraged, the boys yelled more loudly and lewdly, and Wanda started tugging at her arm. "Come *on*, Mom!" She knew the boys from school. Finally, Wanda's mother put her hands on her hips, looked up and shouted, "If you boys don't cut that out, I'm going to come up there and *rape* you." They shut up, abruptly. Wanda cried from embarrassment then, but when she tells the story now, she laughs so hard that she has to go to the bathroom.

I HAD BEEN seeing Jake for a year when his mother announced her second visit. It was close to Mother's Day. After we hung up the phone with her, my left eyelid swelled up immediately. The first time I met her, I had gotten a rash all over my upper arms and inner thighs.

She pinched my shoulder when she saw me. "The weight looks good on you," she said. I wasn't aware that I had accumulated weight, and when we ate lunch together, I ordered a cheeseburger and thought Fuck it.

That night Jake wanted to have sex, but I wondered if he was thinking about his mother, too. So we held hands as he slept and I didn't. With my other hand, I pinched the skin over my stomach. I thought of that old commercial, "Can You Pinch an Inch?" I pinched many inches, then lay in bed with pinch-bruises tingling on my skin.

The next day, we picked up Jake's mother at her hotel. In the lobby she suggested that I take Jake's last name, "just in case." His last name is Holtzenweiser. Jake asked her, "Are you serious?" She tilted her head on her neck like an injured bird. "It was good enough for me," she said.

I had plucked some eyelashes out of my left eye in the attempt to reduce the swelling. I plucked a few too many. Jake's mother asked, "What happened, a kitchen fire?" She was sympathetic, so I said yes. Jake wrapped a strong arm around me and announced that he had bought twenty lottery tickets. "We've all got it made," he said.

Jake's mother checked out of her hotel the last night of her visit and stayed at our place. Making dinner, I pulled baked olives out of the hot oven. I forgot to put the mitts on first. I managed to deposit the sizzling glass pot safely on the stovetop before running to the freezer and grabbing the ice cube trays. Jake pulled at my hands and told me to let him see. They were white and already blistered.

Jake's mother wrapped them in clean dishrags and taped them shut with duct tape. This felt worse, then better. Jake fed me dinner with a fork. His mother pretended that this was ordinary.

Later, I heard them talking in the next room while I lay in bed. I couldn't hear their words, but I knew that they were talking about me from their voices. I did hear "poor thing," the one thing I was supposed to hear. I translated it into Spanish, then Japanese. *Pobrecita. Kawaiso.*

The day Jake's mother left, I watched him make sandwiches for her plane ride. He sliced Havarti cheese, tomatoes, avocados, and then stuffed sprouts in the cracks. She packed her dirty socks into neat rolls.

She started to kiss me good-bye at the door, but I was beginning a bad cold and didn't want to infect her. My nose itched and my eyes were watering. How much more of this can I take, I thought. We walked her outside.

"Bye, Mary Margaret," I said as she walked down the sidewalk to her rental car.

"Call me Mom," she said. I waved. She wasn't my mother. My mother sent me Water Pik attachments for my birthday if she remembered, which she didn't that year. My mother said that I was her least favorite child, although I was her only child. My mother said "Don't call me I'll call you" and didn't.

When Jake's mother called, safely home, we said that I was fine now. We pretended that this was true.

However, eyelid swollen, hands wrapped in gauze, sneezing

on the couch, I thought about how my body comes from some-body's body. This is what's true. Yet impossible.

A FEW MONTHS after he left, my stepfather came back for a few weeks. My mother stopped sleeping and spent a lot of time doing laundry. My stepfather called me Liar. "Hi, Liar. How was school today?" When I told him "Fine," he said, "Sure it was."

One evening he made a lot of noise reading the newspaper. He kept hitting it in the middle to make it stand straight up in the air, and when it buckled over, he swore and slapped it against the arm of the sofa. I tried to concentrate on my home-work at the kitchen table, but made the mistake of saying a vocabulary word aloud, trying to memorize it. I think the word was "infantile." My stepfather sprang off of the sofa and charged toward me. He grabbed my arm, pushed me through the kitchen past my mother and out the back door.

About six inches of snow lay on the ground. I had no shoes or socks on my feet. They were already hurting, beginning to numb in the snow. I looked through the kitchen window at my mother standing inside. She looked back at me through the glass. My stepfather stood next to her and said something in her ear. She put her fists on her hips. He left the room. At first, I was worried that she'd accidentally cut herself with the knife still gripped in one fist. Without realizing it, my own fists rose to my own hips. We watched each other, mirror images. She laughed then, slowly, as I shivered in the snow. I could no longer feel my feet, what I was standing on. We stood there and stared at each other until I realized that I wasn't standing on anything at all.

WANDA'S MOTHER called me at work two months after the abortion. Her voice was loud. I heard the same siren in both of my ears, the one attached to the receiver and the one hanging in the air. "Where are you?" I asked her.

"I'm in the lobby of your office building," she said. "How about lunch?"

"Nancy, it's nine-thirty in the morning."

"I'll wait here. They have nice chairs," she said. "When's your lunch hour? I don't want to set you off schedule."

I hurried downstairs to see her. She wore a pink kimono-dress and balanced a wrapped present on her barely exposed knees.

"Happy happy day," she said.

I opened it right there in the lobby, striped paper drifting to the floor. It was a straw hat with purple plastic grapes dangling from one side.

"It's for your head," she said and fell off her heel, suddenly. She smiled, drunk.

Down the street, over coffee served in a bowl and *beignets*, she began to sniffle.

"She won't talk to me, Wanda won't," she said. She pushed at her long hair, distracted. It stayed where she pushed it, as if underlaid with wires.

"What's the matter?" I asked again.

"She doesn't like my house," she muttered. "She doesn't like my boyfriend. She doesn't call him by name; she calls him by number. I think he's Number 35. What could that mean? Oh, I know. She's cruel, she's a Nazi, I brought a cruel Nazi into this world."

"She's not a Nazi, Nancy," I said, nearly mixing the two words up.

"Of course not," she snapped. "She's Jewish."

She was sobering up a bit and settling into her hangover. She wore a real cameo on a chain around her neck.

"These are good," she said, picking up a *beignet* dusted with powdered sugar.

I bit into one and inhaled sugar, instantly sputtering and coughing. I tried to hold the coughs while I drank coffee, but my diaphragm shuddered against itself and I blew bubbles into the cup. Wanda's mother walloped me on the back with a well-conditioned palm.

"Snap out of it," she said and I did, suddenly.

"Sorry," I said.

"Breathe out when you eat," she told me.

"The whole time?"

"Yes."

"But when do you breathe in?"

"When you're not eating," she said.

"Uh huh."

Suddenly, I looked at her worn face. It was too late for me. And for her.

"You snap out of it, too," I told her, a little too late for context.

She left, as she had the right to do. As soon as she left, there was loss, and there was hunger. I am thirty already, I thought. Thirty. I sat alone at the table for a long time before I finally ate both of our breakfasts, eggs Benedict and trout fried in caper sauce, breathing out the whole time.

BUT SOMETIMES I think of that last time I saw her, my own mother. Together we visited her mother, Grandma Eloise. My grandmother had experienced a succession of bad men, from her husband who called her "slut" and carried a knife to bed to keep her in line, to her brother who flipped a gun in her face and told her to get out of her own house.

Now my grandmother had cataracts and glaucoma. She usually just sat all day in a chair faced away from both the window and the television set. She also had Alzheimer's but recognized some voices, not mine. My mother's voice sliced through the stale afternoon. It glanced off the rusted legs of furniture and the ceramic angels rimmed with dust.

"Guess who can't even wash her own dishes?" my mother said. "Guess who can't manage to keep her drawers clean?"

"Me, me," said my grandmother.

My mother's mouth formed a tightly pressed smile as she slapped the frozen lasagna onto a cutting board. My grandmother flinched at the noise.

I put my hand on my grandmother's shoulder, but it gave at the pressure like bread dough.

On the way home, my mother clasped her gloved hands above the steering wheel.

"I can't believe you did all that," I said.

"All what?"

"What if I do that to you when you're old?" I asked her. "How would you feel?"

She shrugged.

"What happened to you?" I asked.

"What do you mean?" She looked down at her thin coat, her lap.

"How did you get so bitter?"

Her face pursed up. "Listen to you, the big pop-psychologist." Her voice caught in her throat.

Thinking she was hurt, I lowered my voice. "Is it because of your marriage?"

"You're unfit to talk about my marriage. You're the reason I'm alone today."

Staring at the mile markers and the dead scenery, I heard myself say, "You're no kind of mother. You're not my mother."

I turned my head to look at her. Tears poked out of the corners of her eyes, catching in the wrinkles. I was so sorry. And I wasn't sorry at all. Behind her head, the world shot past too quickly for me to register it. Then it stopped as she pulled over and parked on the side of the road. She left the car running as she took off her gloves.

She grabbed my left hand and aligned it with hers, palms facing us. They were perfectly identical—like twin maps. Life line, love line, the same creases in the thumbs. The crooked forefinger. All the same lines and cracks waiting to happen.

"Ha," she said. I shook my head and tried to pull my hand away. She just gripped it tighter. She turned toward me quickly. Her warm breath pushed against my face until I thought I would faint.

"If I'm not your mother," she asked, "then who the hell are you?"

Her First Earthquake

———

It's not what you do—
it's how you do it.

—Mae West

The sixth grade gym class watched Emily's balance beam routine. It had no grace or reason besides the covering of space from here to there. Another dip, a hurried somersault. The black leotard sagged against her chest and stomach. Her breasts had yet to master their training bra, and the rest of her hadn't yet learned to negotiate the ground, the odd angles of walls, the bruises of doors.

Then the class scurried to the wall. Emily nearly stopped and watched. The kids crouched down. They covered their heads. Emily thought they were disgusted by her performance, so she tried harder. Dipping, wobbling and leaping, doing somersaults and jumps on the hard wooden railing.

Then it was easy. Her foot found the wood and gripped where it touched. She couldn't fall. She found perfect balance on her toes. Emily looked up with a smile in the middle of a jump and saw the world heaving and bucking against its own weight. The free weights leaping from their stands. Floor mats shimmying across the room. The ground shaking, easy, loose. Emily stood on her hands.

A high window smashed to pieces. Glass whirled in the designs of tears, of ice. Everything that would happen to everyone else was spelled out like tea leaves, or the patterns of bones. Broken glass cut all around her, except for where she had already landed without noticing. With her arms up in the air, small feet suddenly firm on the dancing floor.

Impersonators

———

I used to be Snow White,
but I drifted.

—Mae West

I met Anna working at a real estate firm uptown. We were both long-term temps—they didn't replace us, and neither of us could commit to a full-time job of such drudgery. We mostly typed and stuck labels on envelopes. The job was unbearable except for the tremendous opportunities to steal office supplies. At least they let us smoke. "Smoking ruins your smile, ladies," our boss would say and head toward his office for a nap or something.

"I'm not a lady, I'm a woman," Anna called down the hall after him. Then a muttered, "So bite me."

We usually took our lunches at the same time and chomped our peanut butter sandwiches in unison. I spent the time imagining what my life would be like in five years. This was so far from where I wanted to be. When I was young, I had wanted to be the first female president of the United States. When I told my mother I was worried that some other girl would get there first, she had said, "Don't worry about that. At all. Ever."

Anna seemed uninterested in everything, including me, but some days I ventured to ask her random polite questions. Anna just stared ahead, chewing bleakly. Sometimes she answered, but the answers were such obvious lies, I stopped asking. For example, when I asked where she was from, she said, "Kuala Lumpur." When I asked what she had brought for lunch, she said, "Head of goat."

At that time, Anna had thick, coarse, Barbie-Doll hair. Always perfect, bouncy. She walked in one morning with a new hairstyle. I said, "I like your haircut."

She ripped the whole head of hair off and twirled it in her fingers a few times. My eyes followed the hair, searching for her face in the empty air beneath it. Then I slowly turned my eyes back to her head at the top of her neck where it should be, her eyes glinting there, her own hair red and fine as a fawn's.

"It's a wig," she said and jammed it back on her head. She dragged on her cigarette, blew smoke at me and grinned. I started typing again. My hands were shaking.

At lunchtime, I asked Anna why she wore wigs.

"Chemotherapy," she said.

I touched my brown lunch bag. Then I said, "Bullshit. I think you wear them because you think they're funny and because you can scare people. I bet you wish you had false teeth, too."

I thought she'd get angry, but she smiled and then laughed. Her laugh was all throat, like Peppermint Patty.

A few days later, she started asking my opinion on things. Not work-related things.

"Who was worse—Pol Pot or Ronald Reagan?" Or: "Why does brie have that white stuff around it?"

Anna and I started doing things together, like we were men. We went to a hockey game. We skated, hiked, went to lunch. Then she asked me to help her move, and it was settled. Friendship, or at least something that looked like it.

"LISTEN," Anna said. "Look."

One man leaned over the restaurant table and said, ". . . so, Rob, I think you're wonderful. And I want to have your baby." The two men stared at each other.

The one man, Rob I guess, said, "I'm flattered. But I date women."

Anna groaned and threw her head back. "How could he turn down a proposal like that?"

The other man poked at his place mat with one finger and said that he understood.

"I don't know," I said. "Isn't that sort of thing nonnegotiable?"

"Have you ever been with a woman?"

"Well, I kissed a woman," I said. "Sort of." Technically, no. In college I made pizzas in the basement of a bar. Sometimes I worked with Hailey, who fascinated me because she told me she had a recycle symbol tattooed directly above her anus.

One day while I was in the cold room and Hailey was watching the ovens, she glanced around, then picked up my Coke can. Hailey carefully fit her lip to the print my lipstick had made on the metal. She didn't drink, just matched up our lips and put the can down. I watched through the chrome mirrors, foot raised midway through a step, holding a handful of cold pepperoni.

"No, not really," I now said.

"Neither have I," Anna said. She leaned in until I could smell her perfume. "But I can picture it. Can you?"

"Mostly yeah. Except for journeying to the dark planet."

"I could do that."

"Could you?"

"Well, I don't know." We both turned toward the sad man at the next table, trying to chew his hamburger. Then he looked at us, and we frowned at each other.

"It's hard trying to get what you need from men," I said, sipping my coffee.

"Yeah."

"Maybe it's impossible."

"Who needs them? My answering machine is more communicative than any man I've ever dated. In fact, I'm going to invent an answering machine that'll throw sultry come-ons at me when I walk through the door— 'Hey, baby, you look like something I dreamt up last night, great legs, give me a little sugar, and by the way, you have three messages. One is new.'"

We laughed. "So," she said. "What happened with Noah?"

Anna had introduced us at a party, saying, "This is Noah. You two would like each other for some reason." Then she walked off to talk to a blond soccer referee.

I talked to Noah that whole night, mostly because I liked his name. My first crush was named Noah—he was color-blind, and in kindergarten class he colored everything wrong. The sun was red. Hair was purple. The sea was golden. I loved him.

This Noah was a consultant for a home shopping network. We hit it off, I think—at least, we knew some of the same books.

Our first date had been interesting. "When we left the movie theater, he invited me over for drinks. First he kissed me for a while on the couch. Then he leaned back and asked me for a blow job."

"Really." Anna didn't seem surprised. She bit into her burger.

"No, he didn't ask. He said, 'I'd like a blow job,' like he was ordering a sandwich."

"Did you?"

"What?"

"Give him one."

"No!"

"I would've. You have to respect that kind of honesty."

"He wasn't being honest. He was being selfish."

"Well, what's the difference?" Anna asked. "Anyway, did you have a nice time?"

"Being honest is selfish?"

"Sometimes." Anna pulled fiercely at her red hair with her slim fingers. I had a sudden urge to grab her chin. My hand jerked out, then stopped. We both stared at it.

*　　*　　*

ON MY SECOND date with Noah, he pulled me close and hugged me for a long time when I got into his car. We said all those things like, "You smell good," and "It's so great to see your face," etc. All the things you say when you're in love, but now we were saying them because we had already been through love with other people, and we were proving to ourselves that we could say these things without them meaning anything. This is what love does to you—you end up canceling yourself out.

We drove to the restaurant since Noah hated walking. As he circled around the block for a parking space, I tried to be entertaining.

"Is that a stick shift or are you just glad to see me?"

"Wocka wocka. What did you do today?"

"Worked. On my lunch hour I called Victoria's Secret and asked them, 'Who's Victoria and what's her secret?'"

"What did they say?"

"There is no secret. There is no Victoria."

"You're surprised."

"Yeah. Well, no. I thought maybe it had something to do with Queen Victoria."

Noah finally parked about four blocks from the restaurant, La Estrellita. My apartment was five blocks from the restaurant.

Over dinner, Noah said, "As a lover, I think I'm really thorough."

By our third round of margaritas, he taught me how to play Six Degrees to Kevin Bacon. "Name an actor."

"Woody Allen."

"Woody Allen was in *Annie Hall* with Diane Keaton, who was in *Crimes of the Heart* with Jessica Lange, who was in *The Postman Always Rings Twice* with Jack Nicholson, who was in *A Few Good Men* with Kevin Bacon. How many was that?"

"Five, I think. Three."

"It helps if you remember just a few connections. Like Jack Nicholson or Meryl Streep." Noah was slightly drunk. He was absolutely charming, flashing his black eyes and leaning across the table. "You're a knockout. Why did you agree to come out with me?"

I was surprised. I hadn't considered it—not going out with him. He called, so I went. I said, "You came highly recommended." This was actually a lie.

"Anna's a sensational chick."

"She's not a chick."

"What is she?"

"A woman."

"Girls are chicks. Men are cats."

"Cats eat chicks."

Noah stroked my jaw with one finger and said lazily, "Don't be stupid."

Everything stopped for me. My dinner swam in its brown gook. I put my hand on my leg. "You called me stupid."

"I urge you to take that in its proper context," Noah said.

This is why I went out with him again: in Japan, they have a phenomenon called the Christmas cake. *Kurisumasu keku.* People buy elaborately decorated cakes for Christmas. All December long, there are cakes in every bakery, every market. Then on the twenty-fifth, Christmas day, you can walk all over Tokyo and you won't find a single one. The storekeepers have thrown them all away. Nobody wants them anymore, not even for free. In Japan, a twenty-five-year-old woman is called a Christmas cake.

BESIDES WORKING with her, I spent most of my free time with Anna, learning about her. She loved tea and had a fantastic memory for names. She said, "I remember throwing a whole cup of Earl Grey all over Alexei Josephs-Berger." Or Prina Stokalosa. Maxwell Buterakis. Ezekiel Mullarkey.

Anna said, "You, your imagination stops where your opinions begin."

She laughed at me for worrying about aging. But she had good cheekbones, and I didn't. I laughed at her when she worried about time. Her favorite holiday was Daylight Saving Time.

She could type fifty words a minute with two fingers. She filed her projects under W ("Waste of my talents, Utter"), B ("Boring"), and BB ("Bearable-Boring").

On Anna's eighteenth birthday, one of her friends had given her edible underwear. She didn't go on a single date for over a year. Anna said that eventually she got tired of waiting and ate them herself.

"They were getting hard," she said.

Anna's mother taught her to say, "I'm a liberal Democrat with socialist leanings" when she was five. Anna inherited her strange way of looking at the world from her mother. Once in the car, we passed the McDonald's Play Place and Anna said, "To go in there, you have to be small, and you have to have socks." This is what I mean about Anna.

But she had faults. She put her decrepit cat to sleep because he shed too much. Once she hit me in the face with a donut when I said that I liked Julia Roberts.

Anna showed me how to fold paper into the shape of a crane. "Blow into its butt," she said when we were through. It inflated into a gawky, sharp-edged bird. I tried to figure out how to do it again by unfolding it step by step, but all I got was creased paper. I couldn't get to that place where Anna was. I didn't know what I offered her in return then; still don't. Maybe it was . . . No.

I INVITED them both over for dinner, Anna and Noah. I poached salmon and served it over smoked Gouda polenta. I baked a cake and carved a peace symbol into the icing. Then I smoothed it over and cut into it.

Anna and Noah had met on a hike. He had followed her down the mountain saying, "Hey, um, miss, um, hey." She kept walking, annoyed. It turns out that she had dropped her keys.

Now, I tried to eat over the din.

"Affirmative action is just another way to screw white men." Noah stuck a finger in his mouth. "I say let it all settle out naturally."

"Naturally? Is it natural that white men steal all the power and do everything they can to keep it at the expense of—"

"Do you believe in Darwin?"

"—underprivileged classes, ethnicities and genders? Yes. Darwin, yes, of course, what do you think I am, an idiot?"

"Well, just think of it as survival of the fittest."

"Survival of those unburdened with a conscience or sense of social responsibility."

"It *is* social responsibility to place the most qualified candidates in the highest positions." Noah leaned back and then almost fell over, since he was sitting on a stool. Then he stared at Anna's breasts, which were resting on the table because Anna was leaning forward so hard.

"Then why are those 'qualified candidates' usually white males?"

"Because—"

"Do you think that white men are naturally superior?"

"No, I think—"

"Or is it that we're naturally inferior?" Anna tapped her lips with her fingertips.

"Can I finish a sentence?" Noah locked his hands together and rested them near his plate. His wrists looked hairier than usual.

I said, "Can we eat here? I mean, I baked this fucking cake."

They both looked at me and then started to eat in earnest.

As I ate, I thought about how Noah's favorite book was *The Fountainhead*. "Except for the rape part," he had said. I thought about how he had given me an earring made out of one of the pins from his knee surgery when he was sixteen.

I realized that I had told Anna too much. Her disapproval hurt me in a strange way. Noah seemed helpless, like the strange child on the playground that nobody wanted on their kickball team. Anna kept rolling her eyes to herself. I felt angry with her; she was always so uncompromising, so absolute. Judging me, everything. I made a muffled sound. She and Noah both glanced at me, chewing. I watched their jaws move up and down in unison without their realizing it.

After a time, Anna held her fork aloft in the air. A small lump of cake trembled on the tines. "I think I get it."

Noah and I looked up from our plates.

"You can't *have* it and eat it too. Get it? I'm thirty-one and just now I get it."

We continued looking, forks paused.

"Like, *having* it, you know? Not just having it around. Keeping it. Yours."

I went back to eating. Noah stared at Anna as she muttered to herself, "*Have* it."

I ONCE MET a middle-aged woman named Lillian Budge who ran a sewing machine store. Her desk was by the storefront so she could watch the passersby while she balanced the books. Her gold nameplate faced the street. Lillian Withers Budge, in curly lettering.

One day, a strange man entered the store, jingling the bell tied to the front door. Everyone looked up, because men rarely went in for sewing machines. He was barrel-chested, with an attractive, open face. He walked directly up to Lillian's desk and stuck out his strong hand. "Budge?" he asked.

She nodded, shaking his hand.

He pointed to his own chest and said, "Mudge."

They hyphenated their names. It was just that simple.

"I want that," I told Anna, blowing on my hands to warm them.

"You want to be Strauss-Mouse?"

I was helping Anna run her yard sale. I was in charge of refolding clothes and pricing items for Spanish speakers. "*Cincuenta centavos, señora. Gracias.* No, but I want something organic like that."

"The O-word. Hey, where are you going with that?" A blond man was sneaking away with a lampshade in his hand. "That's a buck, mister." Anna strode over. He stopped and opened his wallet.

"Stealing at a yard sale," Anna said when she came back to stand next to me, hands clasped behind her back. She shook her little red head and hunkered into her gray sweater like a turtle. Her cheeks were splotched pink.

It was cold out, but the yard was mobbed with people, some who were obviously yard sale "regulars" because they nodded at each other, or bragged about what they had bought for five bucks, for ten cents. "A real coral cameo, twenty-five cents." "A Leica camera. Four dollars. Worth three hundred when I fix the shutter."

I told Anna, "Save me that pair of black boots," and clumped inside to go to the bathroom. Pulling down my jeans and sitting on the toilet, I noticed the purple patterns on the surface of my chilly knees. I stood and pulled up my pants. It occurred to me that nobody was interested in this, in what I did. I washed my hands, made tea for Anna and myself, and joined her outside.

"Wouldn't it be nice to feel like someone really gave a damn? Like something or other was destiny?" I asked Anna.

"I do feel like something or other is destiny."

"I used to think it was destiny with Alex," I said.

"Wasn't he the one who used to sing, 'I am woman, hear me roar . . . Meow.'"

It was true. Alex had also trained me to say, "So, do you think that the Broncos will make it to the Superbowl this year? Think Elway's got it in him one more season?" He used to nudge his friends and tell me, "Say it, honey," and I did. When the Broncos actually did win the Superbowl, I watched the television in horror as my neighbors hooted through the apartment walls, the floorboards.

Now Alex is engaged to a woman named Francesca. I told Anna and she said, "What is that? A coffee?"

I laughed. "So," Anna asked, rubbing her hands together to warm them, "how are things going with Noah?"

"He thinks I'm a hole."

"Does not. How could he?"

"He's just interested in that one thing."

"What are you interested in?"

"A few things. Three, maybe. I don't know. Dating is weird."

"It's like visiting Mars twice a week. When are you seeing him again?"

"Tomorrow."

Anna blew some air out of her nose. Well, she snorted, it could be called that.

"A little sick of Noah," she said.

"Me too." Actually, not really. On our last date, he had given me a black-eyed Susan, picked from the median of a state highway. He nearly caused an accident by braking suddenly and pulling over to the shoulder.

"Noah is," Anna announced, chin up, "a paper plate."

"I slept with him last night."

I listened to what I thought she was thinking. About how I deserved better, all that crap. I answered her in my head. Find me better, Anna. We both watched a man load Anna's rocking horse into his pickup.

"Why did you sleep with him?" she asked, voice casual.

I considered. "He puts his hand on my knee in public places. And he's got his own ideas, his own points of view. I like that. He smiles at me when I'm not even looking at him. I catch him at it when I turn my head. He says that when he commits to a woman, that's it."

"Has he committed to you?"

"Not so much, no."

Someone held up a big purple blanket. "Four dollars," we called out in unison. Anna frowned.

"I don't know, Anna. My sunglasses have outlasted any of my relationships."

Anna held out her hand. "Let me see."

I put the sunglasses in her hand, and she held them up to the light. She squinted at them, then handed them back.

"Nice," she said.

We were quiet for a few minutes, until Anna turned to me. "So, how was he?"

I thought a minute, picking at a rag rug. Anna was counting her money. I struggled between truth and loyalty. Then, between two loyalties. Anna looked up and smiled with all her teeth.

"He was okay," I said.

She nodded.

"Just," I added.

NOAH THREW a party to celebrate his dog's twelfth birthday. I stood by while he played with the dog. Noah rubbed his belly. "Oh yeah, that's a good puppy, Uggy, Uggy-boy." White dog hair was already scattered all over my black party dress. I watched, smiling, until I got jealous. I thought, Why isn't he like that with me? Then I realized why. Because I'm not a dog.

Anna was opening beer bottles with a tabletop. She had it down—with one quick karate chop, the cap flew off somewhere and the bottle breathed steam. She flashed a smile at me.

I thought, She knows all my good things.

I wandered toward the food table and picked at a piece of cheese, cut with a cookie cutter in the shape of a dog bone. Noah started talking to some woman who leaned against the wall as if she was scared. I could tell that he liked that by the way he moved his shoulders back and forth. The woman slid a slender hand into her purse and pulled out a business card. Noah glanced at me.

I looped my arm through Anna's and we wandered into the kitchen for more alcohol. We found a bottle of blended Scotch. I reached above her head for glasses.

Anna grabbed me by the shoulders and kissed me. Savage and light. One of my hands was still in the air, holding a glass. Her hands were thin and strong. She put them in my hair. I found my other hand reaching for her breasts. Like mine, but different. Everything—like me, but different.

After a long time I stepped back. My knees buckled a little. Anna touched her lips, steadied herself against the counter.

"We're friends," I said, voice shaking. I heard Noah laugh in the next room.

"Listen," Anna said, her hands back on my shoulders. "Listen. I think I'm in love with you. I am. It's love. You know how I know? Last time I was at your house, I started petting your gym shoe when you were in the bathroom. Just like it was a dog. I swear."

"Anna. Anna."

She blushed. "It's just that I know all about you. Your tastes, your politics, although I don't agree with that stuff about Oliver North. It's not enough for me anymore."

"Well, what is enough?" I got angry, mostly because I didn't know how else to get her hands off my shoulders. "Why do you always opt for the hard way?"

"It's always hard."

"Yeah, but changing your sexuality? Going for your best friend? Come on, Anna. Either one of those things is enough to drive you to the edge."

"It's better than staying away from the edge just because you're afraid." She put her fists on her hips.

"I'm not afraid."

"You liked it when I kissed you! You kissed me back!"

"I did not!"

"Yes you did!"

"I don't want to deal with this." I put my hands on my head, near my ears. The music boomed through the kitchen walls. Someone broke a glass in the next room. A toilet flushed.

She lowered her voice. "It was inevitable. Just think about how much time we've been spending together."

"But you choose, Anna. You choose who you love. You choose what you fight for."

"I don't. Right now, I can't think of anything I wouldn't fight for."

Her eyes were as hard as water when you land on it from a place so high in the air that it's no longer water. It's something else, something blue that will swallow your whole body and life in an eruption, then show its rigid surface again without a blink.

ANNA DIDN'T show up at work. I licked envelopes by myself. Maybe I'm pregnant, I thought. Maybe I'm sick. Maybe I have throat cancer.

When my boss asked me to please paper clip all relevant materials together in the future, I answered, "Where's Anna?"

"We'll have her replacement this afternoon."

"She quit?"

"She didn't have to quit. She's a temp. So are you."

Anna's replacement came in after lunch. He was a man with black curly hair who kept talking about his fiancée until I said, "You think you're the only one who's ever been engaged? Do you really think that this is an original situation?"

I called Anna that night. "Why did you leave me alone there in hell?" I had to swallow mid-sentence and my voice made this chugging sound.

"I can't just brush over things like you do. I can't not feel things." But she sounded like she didn't feel anything at all.

"How are you?"

Anna didn't answer.

"What are we going to do?"

"I don't know. I'm totally adrift here. I'm thinking, what's the point to human relationships anyway? And if they're futile, what's the point to living?"

"You're scaring me."

"Don't worry."

"Sure."

"I have this little trick. Every time I consider suicide I think, I can kill myself, or I can go to Puerto Vallarta."

I laughed, listening to my laughter in the phone's echo.

"I had this dream last night," Anna said. "I dreamt that I made you a seven-course meal. I even remember some of the dishes—carpaccio, apricots stuffed with gorgonzola cheese, some soup made out of Chardonnay. I guess I went to bed hungry. Anyway, I served it to you on matching white dishes, poured wine, and sat down next to you. I put my hand on your knee. You turned to me and said, 'Can I get it to go?'"

This hurt. "I dreamt about you last night too."

"Yeah? What?"

I didn't tell her. How I was chasing her and chasing her until

I finally caught her in a bright green field. When I caught her, I couldn't hold her—my grip slipped, and she was changing into something else. A creature entirely too big. And completely unmanageable.

ONCE I MET a female impersonator at a party. She wasn't a female impersonator all the time—mostly onstage, and sometimes when she went out or hung around the house. When in drag, she went by Frieda. In men's clothing, Fred.

That night she was wearing a leather bra and PVC pants. I thought about PVC and how if Frieda left those pants around and a baby started chewing on it, the baby could develop liver and kidney damage. Frieda said that she didn't have kids yet. When she did, she said, she'd get rid of the pants.

Sometime later in the evening we attacked the cold fried chicken in the appetizer baskets together, sharing a bottle of ouzo someone swiped from the liquor cabinet. Our lipsticks blended together on the bottle's rim—black and red. Frieda said, "I have this problem."

Frieda told me that when she's performing onstage, she knows just what to do. She sings, dances in high glittery heels, shimmies her artificial breasts. She's brassy, all woman. She's a superstar.

But offstage, when nobody's watching, she gets confused. She'll snap her fingers and say, "Oh, nuts!" while encased in black leather stud gear on her way home from the theater. She rearranges her crotch and spits when she's wearing a negligee in the dressing room. She dates boys as a boy, boys as a woman, women as a boy, women as a woman.

I said that it was easy for her. She had options. She really did straddle the line. It's different when you're a biological woman and you don't even know what that means. Besides, she only had to deal with it all on a part-time basis, always on her own terms. "What's at stake, really?" I asked her. "Very little."

Yes, she said. Until you fall in love.

NOAH TOOK me to a seafood restaurant and then explained that he maxed out all his credit cards so could I float him?

I inhaled quickly. Anna sat at the bar, drinking something brown. I pointed a finger.

"There's Anna," I said.

Noah pulled my chair out and steered me over to the bar where Anna was sitting cross-legged on a stool. Noah put his big hand on her shoulder. I almost said, "Don't touch her," but then Anna swiveled around.

"Oh," she said.

I immediately thought of my clothes—black dress, silly shoes, all for Noah. But Anna's eyes were on her drink, not me. Noah didn't say anything, just smiled and stood there. I tried to say something, but it was impossible, like starting to peel an orange with bitten nails.

Finally Anna said, "Well, next time make an appointment because you really put a crimp in my plans when you just drop in like this."

"Oh, Anna," I said.

"I like your shirt," Noah said. Anna and I both turned and stared at him, then rolled our eyes at each other. Then she remembered that she hated me more than she hated Noah and said, "I hate this shirt." It was a dark purple shirt, knitted raw silk with tight sleeves. The color brought out her eyes. I had given it to her for her birthday.

"You do not," I said. "You love it. You said so."

"Don't. It smells funny."

"Then why are you wearing it?"

"Here. Take it back."

She tugged it over her head and off in about one second flat. She tossed it in my face. It looped around my head, smelling like soft sweat and honeysuckle. I yanked it off. Anna's stomach buckled slightly above the waistline of her miniskirt. She stared at the floor, as if she weren't half-naked in a restaurant, as if it were all so far away.

"Keep your shirt on, lady," the bartender said, carefully setting a bowl of soup on the bar. Then he held his hand out for the shirt. I gave it to him. He handed it back to Anna, and it traveled in this small triangle. She held it against her blue bra for a second. Then she pulled the shirt back on. She picked up a spoon, her small red head bent against me.

After we sat down at our table again, Noah said, "I know what's going on."

"Good, then why don't you let me know? Because I'm pretty confused."

"I'm trying to be sensitive about this." He was, and I felt warm toward him for a moment. He was twisting the tip of his napkin into a fine point. I looked over at Anna, who dropped her napkin into her lap. It rested there, all bunched up.

"It was just one kiss," I said.

"What do you mean, a kiss?"

"It just happened once."

Noah furrowed his brow for a second, then his face cleared. "What? *You* and Anna? I thought this was about me." Noah turned his face away, but his body stayed the same, slouched back. "Great. Fantastic."

Anna was trying to swallow her soup. She pressed her fingers against her mouth and tilted her head down toward her lap. She said something to the bartender. It sounded like "Check," but it might have been "Chicken."

Noah asked, "What do you want, anyway?"

Anna put her face in her hands, her palms pressed against her eyes, then pulled money from her pocket.

"What do I want?" I echoed.

Anna stood up then—beautiful and wild, her little body tensed for flight. Stay, I wanted to say. Wait. My mouth opened.

"I want Anna," I said, before I knew I had said it. Anna turned toward me. Together we listened to the words take shape and grow in the air.

It was like nothing I had ever known before. Anna calls it *vu déjà*—the feeling that you've never been here before. This place where you find yourself—everything has already changed from underneath without warning, like a child that has grown up to look exactly like you, and starts talking back for the first time.

Momentum

———

It's not the men in
your life that counts—
it's the life in your men.

—Mae West

In the movies, he always comes back, the man who can't commit. The woman throws him out, balls his clothes into a suitcase, boxes up his books and lines them outside the door. Sometimes, everything goes out a window—the record collection (he refuses to switch to CDs), the shoes. The dry-cleaned shirts billow on the lawn, grass stains already soaking into the sleeves.

But in those cases, he doesn't come back for a long time, maybe years. No, the possessions must be intact, but just outside the door. The man and woman have a few strained encounters at parties or coffee shops; she loses twenty pounds. She considers suicide after disastrous dates with actuaries and sanitation engineers. He dates a Playboy bunny.

Then he comes back. She welcomes him. They love each other. He gives up his freedom, after she gives up everything else.

A person can live without expectations, it's true. Irene plucked her eyebrows into an expression of surprise; surprised when Tom kissed her, surprised when he said, "This summer we should . . ." At one point, she walked into a supermarket and thought, Imagine that, they have food here.

"Leave him," Irene's friends told her, slowly and repeatedly. To which she wondered and didn't say, But what if he likes it?

No, she had decided that she could keep it going, like a top. She would construct a universe without gravity, without the second law of thermodynamics, without anything else but Irene, Tom, and their possible love for each other.

She knew she was that tough.

THEY HAD been living together for five years when Tom had said over burgers and beer, "I don't know if I want a relationship anymore."

Irene thought it had to be a joke, what with the pleased expression on his face. Then she realized that it was no joke, he just felt pleased about it.

"What do you mean, a relationship? I'm the relationship." Tom continued eating, so she said, "You don't know if you want *me* anymore."

"Your words, not mine."

Irene got up to leave, chewed-up food still in her mouth. Tom left with her, throwing some money next to his plate. It was too familiar, the way he moved to do this. She followed him outside.

"You don't want me," Irene said in a daze. It was beginning to snow.

"I don't know what I want."

"How will you know? When will you know? How did this change?" She was crying already. There are no answers to these questions. They walked without speaking for several blocks.

"How can you be so blasé about this?" Irene asked, her voice thick.

"I'm not."

"What did I do wrong?"

"Will you please say something original," Tom snapped.

Once home, Irene sat on the sofa and cried. Tom disappeared into their bedroom. Irene sobbed louder so he'd hear her and come back to say that it was a mistake. The red flannel sheet they used as a couch cover sopped up her tears.

Through the crying, Irene looked around their apartment. She realized that everything Tom owned was in distinct piles, separate shelves, little escape pods. When had this happened? She didn't know. She remembered that he had wanted to wait before resubscribing for the newspaper, and that he made a special point of doing only his own laundry yesterday, folding it neatly into his dresser drawers.

Then Irene started to hear this noise through her sobs, a chalky pop pop pop sound. She couldn't place it, so she stopped crying to listen. It came from the bedroom. She tried to ignore it, but its irregularity had something familiar about it. She stumbled toward the bedroom, sniffling and hiccupping. The sound grew slightly louder.

Tom sat on their bed, staring into space. Flossing his teeth.

"Get out," Irene said. No, she didn't say it. She wishes she had said it. No, she doesn't.

IN THE BATHROOM at work, before she flushed, an old love note fell out of Irene's pants pocket. It slowly fell into the toilet bowl, on top of the urine and wadded toilet paper. Before she knew what she was doing, Irene reached into the water and grabbed the note, wiping it in with her hands to make sure that the ink didn't bleed.

She stood in the stall with wet hands, looking at this piece of paper. *You're beautiful when you're asleep, see you at 6:00. Love. Tom.* Then she washed her hands in the sink, rinsed the paper carefully, and sniffed it to make sure it was clean. Put it back in her pocket.

Now, when she chose a cup for her tea, Irene thought, should I use the cup we bought together on our two-year anniversary? Or his cup from his old apartment? Would that make him feel smothered? Or like he was sharing? Should I use my old cup with the broken handle? But would that symbolize something to him?

Irene told her friends about this, mostly her long-distance friends. She called them on the phone, and they made up names for Tom, like The Terminator. They said that aliens had landed and sucked the soul out of his body. They made up titles for self-help books, such as *What Do I Do When His Inner Child's a Brat?* Ideas for game shows: "Is He Treating Me Like Shit, or Is It Just My Imagination?" They laughed, but nobody really thought it was very funny. Sometimes that's what's funny.

They gave her chains of advice. "When Jack did that to me, I told him to *get out right now*. That really fixed him."

"Honey, maybe you should be the strong one here. Be his rock."

"When they want to go, you just have to let them go."

"Have you considered an affair?"

Irene cried so much, her eyes became used to tears and no longer swelled up. She could now cry often and gracefully—on the way to the supermarket, in the bathroom during karate class, alone at the table trying to eat her shapeless breakfast. She cried when she saw a vanity license plate that said "Aw Rats." A bumper sticker that said, "Stop Continental Drift."

Irene went out one night with the full intention of picking someone up. Instead, she drank too much and followed a college student to a toga party somewhere. She woke up lying on the ground between two elevators, a contour sheet twisted between her legs.

She came home at four in the morning. Tom didn't wake up when she flopped into bed next to him. Irene stayed awake, watching the window grow brighter. She thought of the world outside, stripped of its passion. She looked at an empty glass, a shoebox; she looked at his once-familiar face.

The next morning, Tom said, "You need to start thinking of us in economic terms. Diminishing returns, opportunity cost. You need to look out for yourself."

Irene told her friends stories of Tom's past devotion. How she once accidentally left her phone off the hook all night when she lived alone. Tom ran all the way to her apartment and climbed up the fire escape. He forced the kitchen window partly open and banged the spaghetti pot against the stove burners until Irene woke up. Tom was so upset and worried about her, his tongue trembled when he licked his lips.

Irene told her friends, "I can stand anything for one more day."

And oh, the sex, the sex now. Brutal. Yet good in a new way, the way they took chunks out of each other, waking with bruises and hickies neither could remember giving or getting. After they fell away to opposite sides of the bed, chests heaving, Tom looked shocked at the things they had done to each other, before glazing over again and falling asleep.

Irene simmered dates in brandy and stuffed almonds into the sticky insides. She rolled these little brown bullets in sugar. Put them in a bowl and watched them disappear day after day, Tom's fingers dipping in and out.

"I'm honestly trying here," Tom said. But he came home later and later, ate, packed up new things and left again for somewhere else.

IRENE HAD left men before. She'd gathered the loose jewelry from the bathroom, picked up the used condoms and split. She's capable.

But in any relationship it's impossible to see the daily braveries. For example: there's this couple at a party. The husband calls his wife "old bag." He tells everyone in the room about a disgusting personal habit she has, such as picking her toenails at the table. He rolls his eyes when she talks. His friends laugh because he does. Her friends laugh nervously, as if it's a joke, as if everyone's on the same side here.

Her friends tell their husbands as they drive home, "I don't know why she won't leave him. That pig." They're relieved to be with their own men, who only have problems with impotency/communication/back hair. Relieved that they don't have to go home to a life of what they have witnessed.

But neither does she, the woman who picks her toenails. At home, she says, "What the fuck were you thinking?" He says, "I don't know," or "I'm a jerk," or worst of all, "Maybe I'm not cut out for this."

She says, "You can do anything." She says, "Talk to me." She watches him lower his head into his spread hands. She touches his shoulder, ignoring his flinch. She says, "I am your friend."

This is bravery, although it's usually called something else.

IN THE STREET Irene once found a loose diamond among the spread scat of glass shards. She held it in her hand like a broken bird until she got home. Then she dropped it in a wineglass and looked at it every few hours. She invited her friend Sue over. Sue pinched the diamond between the tips of a pair of tweezers.

"Worthless," Sue said, "this diamond is so small, it's worthless without a setting."

Irene thought of her diamond amidst mountain peaks and caves. She pictured the diamond tumbling in a river, while it sank intact, facets dimming.

"No, baby," Sue said. "Setting means *ring*."

Toward the beginning of their relationship, Irene had the diamond made into an earring and gave it to Tom. "Happy October," she said. He had said, "What is it, really?" unable to believe that it wasn't glass, that it was real. But she had already checked, pounding it with a crowbar on the sidewalk.

Now she looked at him asleep next to her in bed. He was so helpless in his sleep, with his light brown hair trailing toward his ear like a question mark. Irene wanted to punch him as hard as she could in the mouth. Then she imagined how he would wake up, terrified and in pain, dreaming nightmares. Irene loved him even harder then, with all the remorse of what she hadn't done.

She touched his diamond, the hardest substance on the planet. She gently unscrewed the back of the earring and pulled it out of his ear. She meant to just look at it in the dark, to see if any light would reflect from it. But instead, Irene put it in her mouth and swallowed it so quickly, she barely tasted the metal and dead skin before it scraped down her throat.

In the morning, she woke to Tom tearing the blankets off her body. "My earring. It's gone." He was clutching his ear with one hand while clawing through the sheets with the other.

Irene crawled over to him and drew as close as she could, their knees knocking each other. "It's here." She tried to hold him.

He pushed her away and picked at the ridges in the mattress. "I have to find it." He scraped his nails against the carpet. "It was in my ear when I went to bed, I checked."

Irene pretended to help him look under the mattress and in the pillowcases. After a while, she really did start looking, as if there was something to be found. She felt around the edge of the bed frame and tore a chunk out of the side of her finger.

They stopped looking. "I want to be alone," Tom said.

"I'm here," Irene said. "You idiot. A diamond's a symbol. I'm the real thing." When Tom looked at her, Irene saw from his face that he knew that she had taken it. But no, she wanted to say. I didn't keep it.

Later, he poked a stainless steel stud into the hole in his ear. He would eventually be happier this way, making do. He was from Minnesota, after all. Irene thought about the diamond working its way through her body. It was probably halfway

through her at that point. She felt valuable, holding this small
hard thing inside her for the moment.

TOM DECIDED that a trip together might make things clearer
for him. First Chicago, then Oregon to see his brother. Then
back home to their apartment, where everything would look
comforting by comparison, Irene thought. Or boring.

In Chicago, they ate a lot of Mediterranean food and went to
the zoo. It was chilly and drizzling, so they shared a pair of
gloves, switching hands and pockets every few minutes. They
went to an indoor exhibit to look at the bugs. Tom stood next to
a cage full of *blaberus giganteus:* the Cockroach of the Divine
Face. Irene looked back and forth between Tom and the cock-
roaches.

Tom asked which she liked better, the primates or the great
cats. Irene thought about it, the sweet baby gorilla matching its
hand up to hers against the glass, chewing on its other fist while
the attendant said, "Don't touch." The orangutans gently
scratching each other. Then she told Tom, "Great cats," because
they were sexier, more restless.

They went to the science and technology museum, the whis-
per chamber. Tom stood her on the carpeted platform, then
crossed the long room to the other side and stood on the other
platform.

Tom whispered, "Hi." She heard it right behind her ears, so
close, she could imagine his breath there. Irene closed her eyes
and whispered, "I love you." She swayed in the humming room.
She only heard his breathing, so she said it again, thinking he
didn't hear her. "I love you, I love you." And then, his rustling
voice, "Do you . . . are you hungry? Do you want to get a snack?"
Irene opened her eyes. Tom looked so far away, with one small
foot turned in. His breathing. He looked to the side of the room
at the guard. Irene lost her footing on the platform.

Stepping down, a middle-aged woman was already waiting to take Irene's place. Her husband leaned against the wall, and the woman called out crossly, "Come on, come on." Behind them, another woman herded her children into a line. They punched each other and then looked up at their mother sheepishly.

Tom met Irene off to the side of the room, touched her arm and whispered into her actual ear, "I love you too." Irene was supposed to understand the joke, the joke on purpose.

Outside, the rain had stopped and a full rainbow cleared the sky. They looked at it together, end to end. Irene thought it was the dumbest thing she had ever seen.

Oh, Chicago, Chicago, she thought. But she hadn't left yet.

"Oh, Chicago," Irene said aloud.

Tom said, "You know, I should live here."

As Irene was thinking, *I should live.*

ON THE TINY propeller plane from Bend, Oregon, Irene woke with her head in Tom's lap. Before her eyes were open, she knew she was going to be sick. "I feel sick," she told him. "The turbulence."

"Five minutes until landing," the pilot announced, not by loudspeaker, but by calling softly over his shoulder. Eight people sat in the plane; it was a full flight.

"Just five minutes," Tom said, groping the seat pockets in front of them. He only found one airsick bag. He handed it to Irene, eyes worried. "I need more than one," she said. "That big lunch." Then she began to get sick.

The day before, Irene had hugged the icy side of a ski slope that was too steep for her, as she couldn't ski. "Come on," Tom said. "Just a little more."

Irene fought to stay upright on the slope. She fell down every few minutes. Tom stopped downslope to watch her get up each time.

He said, "You look like one of those plastic clowns that bounce against the floor every time you hit them, then they pop up grinning."

He said, "Why don't you watch your technique? Bend more."

He said, "You just have to keep at it. You're not even trying very hard."

Irene whispered, "I hate you," and tried to get up one more time. Halfway up, she looked at Tom and suddenly changed her mind. Just like that. She sat down in the snow, her skis crossed. "That's it," Irene said. "Right here. This is as far as we go."

It had felt like a test at first, and then she was amazed at how something could stop so suddenly. She was through. Tom looked like a child whose roller coaster ride had ended while he was still upside-down on the tracks, arms raised above his head.

"What do you mean?" he had asked.

"I'm done."

"But you can't just give up. You have to keep trying."

"No," Irene said. And it seemed to be that simple. In fact, it was. She was furious that it was. She unlatched her skis and began to walk down the mountain by herself.

Now, she was throwing up into the bag, which was heavy and beginning to split open at the bottom. Tom placed a magazine in her lap, open. The bag broke, emptying onto the pages of a *Time* magazine article about all those tortured prisoners of war, and the terrorists backed into the hills living on rodents and grasses. Irene kept holding the bag to her face, now merely a funnel. "Please," she said, "ask someone for help."

"It doesn't matter." Tom turned his face away, toward the window. "We're landing."

And they were. Irene hung her head. Her sodden hair banged against her cheek as the plane touched down with a series of jolts.

Irene walked off the airplane after telling the disgusted captain about the state of the upholstery on her seat. Tom was already off the plane, smoking a cigarette, holding his own stomach.

In the airport bathroom, Irene sopped her jeans with wet paper towels. She ducked her head under the spigot. She furiously pumped soap out of the dispenser, then looked at it in her hand as if she had never seen anything like it before.

"Did you spill?" the woman at the next sink asked.

"Yes."

"Looks like you made a mess." The woman looked at Irene's hair, her legs.

"Yes," Irene said, "I made it. I made it. I made it."

The woman left, and Irene did too. Walked out wet and cold, with those words thudding inside her, ruthless as a heart.

WAS IT machismo? Was it love? Was it the splendor of victimhood? The way some women carry a bruise like a fetus? Irene no longer remembered.

Outside a downtown coffee shop, Irene handed Tom the house key. With a grunt he gave her a heavy cardboard box labeled "What She Left Behind." They made the exchange on the sunniest day, so bright that Irene's eyes stung under her sunglasses.

Tom was changed. He was simply some man she had known intensely for five years, nothing more. A man with a bad haircut. She knew the way each hair grew on his head, and this knowledge now seemed so absurd that she wanted to sit down with her head in her hands.

The box was very heavy. "Could you drive me to my new apartment?" Her arms already ached. "It's ten blocks from here. I walked."

"I can't." Tom folded himself like a jackknife into his dented Toyota. "You can carry it yourself."

"I've done that for five fucking years."

"You can do it for the rest of your life, now." He slammed the door.

"Hey!" She banged on his shut window. "You're just a *person*. That's all. There are six billion of you." Tom drove away. Irene stood still for a moment.

When she couldn't carry it anymore, she tried to kick the box down the street, but it was just too heavy. Irene sat on the sidewalk in the dancing shadow of a leafless tree, her purse clunking against her side. She pushed at the box with both legs. It scudded a few inches and then stopped. She thought for a few moments, sitting on the chilly ground. Then she opened the box with a pencil, puncturing the tape.

Irene pulled out hand-weights: 2 lb., 5 lb., 10 lb. She played one of them in her hand. She placed them all on the sidewalk. They rolled downhill a little until they curved off into the dead grass.

She picked up the box again, much lighter. She walked with one hand inside, groping.

A cup with a broken handle. Three bike helmet pads. A Dustbuster filter, used. *The Joy of Sex.* Three key chains. A piece of green candle wax, melted flat. Seven paper clips chained together. Velvet shoes.

Fabric cleaner with a warning on the label: "This product contains a chemical known to the state of California to cause cancer." A bowl that looked like a watermelon. A bookmark that looked like a fish. A stuffed cow to put over a broom handle, so it doesn't look like a broom. To make it look like a cow.

As she picked up each item, she let it fall through her fingers to the sidewalk. All the way home, ten blocks. When she got to her door, she looked behind her. A multicolored Hansel and Gretel trail stretched behind her for years, ultimately stopping where she stood. This is all that's left of us, Irene thought. She felt strangely light and loose, like a violin whose strings have been cut.

Irene dropped the cardboard box. It landed on its corner, then its side. So that anyone passing by could see how empty it was. So that anyone could see the exact spot where she finally lost everything.

The Husbands

————

*There was a time I didn't
know where my next
husband was coming from.*

—Mae West

I like to sleep with other women's husbands. I try not to like this. It's not the healthy thing to do, either mentally or hygienically. I see a shrink. I see a gynecologist. But then I sleep with the husbands anyway.

I started big, with my own sister's husband, Patrick. Sarah had always been the stupider one, the uglier one, and the one who lost her virginity first. It's like I couldn't let her get away with that one. The first time I slept with Patrick, I seduced him in a bathroom at a party. I walked in while he was standing at the toilet.

I slept with my best friend's husband. Norton. This did not make me feel like a woman. I slept with my librarian's husband, while she was at work, counting books. Friends, acquaintances, coworkers. All husbands.

After I started sleeping with her husband, my sister asked if I was seeing anyone special. I said, "Unique, anyway."

Sarah smiled. "What's he like?"

"Oh, you know. Like a man. Male." Sarah kept waiting for more information, so I said, "A mailman."

"Maggie, get serious. Don't you want to find someone? The One?"

"I don't believe in the One."

"Don't you want security?"

I stared at her and then laughed. She laughed, too.

I told Sarah, "I'm the girl in the movies where the guy marries the other, really nice and less slutty girl."

Sarah and Patrick got married when she was twenty-three. I had dated him first, for nine months in high school. He and Sarah dated for the rest of high school and then college. She had never been with another man. "Tell me details," she said, eyes shiny. "I need stories of adventure."

"It's not all that exciting. Probably just like what you and Patrick do," I said.

I live across the street from a halfway house. I wave at the inmates at night ("Hi, guys!"). Squirrels live in my walls, running around in the early hours, hiding nuts or whatever. A previous tenant had once set fire to one corner of my carpet. The refrigerator sounds like Darth Vader. My landlord has a tattoo on his face. It says Jail Sucks.

My sister and Patrick live in a mansion. They have an entire wall of cabinets dedicated to their crystal and china, with display cases for the prettiest plates. They have three Afghan hounds, petulant as cats. Sarah sometimes holds up a tablecloth and says, "Only a hundred bucks! Can you imagine?" She invites me over for dinner and shows me all the things she's bought since she saw me last. While I look at these things, I let the wine pool in the side of my cheek before I swallow it. I'm older than her by two years.

MY SISTER'S name is Sarah Allison Brown. She did not keep her name when she married Patrick. She isn't a beautiful sister, or even a particularly interesting one, but she's mine. Nobody gets to make fun of her but me. I'd kill for her.

I'd also kill her. Growing up, she drove me crazy, so needy and sad. Our parents died in a car crash when Sarah was sixteen and I was eighteen. Our parents were both only children; besides a stray great-aunt, we had nobody at all.

My shrink says that this is why. My shrink says that I'm suppressing latent homosexual desires by instead sleeping with the husbands. She says that I have an extreme fear of intimacy, yet I'm fascinated by it, so I choose to witness it risk-free, by sleeping with the husbands. She says that the husbands represent things to me. Fathers, sons, women, power.

My last real boyfriend, the one I introduced to Sarah, he wasn't a husband. He was an astrophysicist. When I broke up with him, Sarah lightly shook my shoulders, saying, "But there's nothing *wrong* with him."

Sarah told me stories about Patrick. How he wore his socks to bed every night, black ones, even in the summer when the air conditioning was on the blink. How he gave her flowers when he was sorry, only when he was sorry.

Patrick told me stories about Sarah: long, whining stories about how she washed his suit in the washing machine once, or how she baked his birthday cake a day early. Then he'd stop short, saying, "Oh, sorry, she's your sister."

It's hard to love, and it's hard not to. I'm better at the *not* part. Sarah loves enough for both of us. She's one big heart, that thrusting muscle. She's a small animal with eyes on opposite sides of the head, watching all the time, but for only one thing. Danger.

SARAH BOOKED a cruise around the Virgin Islands. "It'll be just the two of us, like sisters."

"Bad idea," I had told her, but she bought my ticket, so I told my boss that I was going to be sick for a week in April.

I'm a makeup artist for opera singers. I like my job—I like the exaggeration. I like to paint an eye to say, Yes. This is an eye. An eye for people with myopia—an eye for those of you in the cheap seats. This is everybody's eye.

Patrick and I got braver. We paid for rooms with his credit

card. I went with him to Texas for the weekend and lounged around the hotel room in my underwear while he met with clients. At night, in his slightly fleshy arms, I said, "I don't want to go on a cruise."

"Maybe you'll meet someone," Patrick said.

I sat up by planting my elbow on his stomach. "Oof," he said. "You're so sexy." He rolled over, exposing a triangle of back hair where his shoulder blades met. It had spread like a fungus since he was a teenager, and he didn't have the courage to wax it, the dexterity to shave it.

Patrick—a quasi-honest man who tried hard, or at least that's how he marketed himself. Sometimes he broke character—rented a porno, didn't bother to recycle, slept with his wife's sister.

Once he was walking down the street, holding a small purple rock to give to his niece, when he saw a fat, dumb squirrel about ten yards away. He threw the rock and beaned the squirrel on the head, perfectly. He felt guilty when he saw the squirrel's face, confused, tottering off toward a tree to figure it out or maybe die. But he was proud of the shot, right on the sloped forehead. He was half in love with that shot, and relived it many times without its consequences. He never told Sarah.

I don't sleep with the husbands for this kind of inside information, or for the compliments, or the attention. I guess I do it because I'm only good at being different. I'm the one that's not the wife, not remotely the wife. Not remotely anyone's wife, ever. That's exactly what I'm good at.

THE CRUISE ship had a tennis court with a big white shell over it, a lounge, a swimming pool, and a bunch of hopscotchy-looking drawings on the deck where you slide a puck with a stick for points and feel very fulfilled about it. The ship got going. We waved good-bye from the deck, even though we had nobody to

wave good-bye to; we had taken a shuttle there. Sarah clutched
a red silk handkerchief and flapped it.

"You've got to be kidding," I said.

"Patrick bought it for me. He said, 'Wave it and think of me,
even though I'm in Duluth.'" She looked at me. "Business trip."

Sarah wouldn't stop pointing out men. "How about that
one? Standing outside the ladies' room? Oh, looks like his wife
just came out. How about that one with the tie?"

"I don't like his teeth."

"His *teeth*, Maggie? What does that matter?"

"You have to be picky in the beginning, because after you fall
in love, you don't care anymore."

"So? Then you're happy, and together."

"God, Sarah. You don't stay that way."

We shared a cubby-sized room with one narrow bed, which
was all Sarah could get on short notice. That night, after dinner
and a mixer that I sat out, Sarah read a book with her back to
me as I lay there, sleepless, watching the light bulb burn so
steadily for something so fragile.

THE FIRST morning, we disembarked for a day at the beach. A
suited boy carried around a sign with a bell on it that said,
"Remember Sunscreen!" Sarah emerged from the room with a
pink straw hat and a cotton dress, the kind with the waist all the
way down by the hips. She stopped when she saw my bikini top.

"You're just wearing that?" she asked. "Your belly button
ring, Maggie. I mean, this is a conservative environment. There
are Republicans everywhere."

I went back for a T-shirt.

The beaches were so beautiful that they looked fake. All
truly beautiful things look fake. I had been to Alaska—fake.
Greece—fake, fake. They look like reproductions of themselves.

Sarah and I lay on our beach towels and slapped lotion on

each other's backs. I felt strange doing that. I realized that I hadn't touched my sister since I was a kid, when we used to play with each other's hair or pick each other's scabs. Now, her skin felt strangely familiar, yet not. Her body had changed in ways that felt like a betrayal. Her thighs had gotten enormous, with puffs of cellulite puckering the backs. The tops of her arms wobbled. We were in our early thirties. I wanted to blow a whistle and make her do pushups.

"This is fun. Isn't it?" Sarah asked.

"Yeah." I watched the ocean.

"I wish we did more sister stuff together."

"What is sister stuff?"

"You know what I was thinking yesterday? I was thinking that we have such different memories of each other, growing up. Like, what I remember, you don't, and vice versa. So when bad stuff happens, the other person doesn't learn from it, they just move on, and you're the one who's left sad or mad or whatever." Sarah picked her tooth with a pinky nail, then looked at the opaque peach polish for chips.

"Are you mad at me for something?" I asked.

"I a little bit resent the way you used to hide my Raggedy Ann doll."

"I didn't do that."

"See?"

Sarah was quiet for a minute, then said, "But you beat up that boy who was making fun of my glasses. You were my hero."

I felt suddenly sick. I rolled over and stared at a plastic bucket until it came into slow focus.

It's not true what they say, that when you lose family, you cling to what remains. No, you weed out the desire. You attack the need for family. It's not a physical need. You replace it, like smoking, with something else, like carrots, or jogging, or even sex.

Still, there is this way of being sisters. There's this way that you laugh at each other's jokes, even when they're stupid. This way of knowing not just what the person is saying, but every single thing underneath it; understanding the placement of the strings on the piano you're playing. I can tolerate it for about ten minutes, and the rest is torture.

ON A CRUISE, there are many, many husbands. I know how to get the husbands. First, there's the look. Like you don't care, which you don't. Shiny clothes help. Men are like crows—they like to pick up shiny things, take them back to their nests and poke at them with their beaks.

You can play the klutz: "Oh, I'm sorry, I bumped into you, is that tie ruined? Let me take care of the dry cleaning, no, I insist, give it to me, you can get a new one in your room, oh, what a nice, nice room, nice bed . . ." Or the concerned neighbor: "Is your wife really seasick? I have the perfect seasick medicine in my room, it's all herbal . . ." Or anything, really, anything at all. They meet you halfway, and walk you home.

At dinner, Sarah and I sat at a round table with a doctor and his wife. The wife was pretty and cloying. Sarah adored her. "That's so very true," Sarah said every time the wife finished a sentence. Or, "I can't wait to tell Patrick about that."

An annoying habit of Sarah's: she thinks about everything twice. Sometimes she'll say something, then mouth the words to herself afterwards. She doesn't know she does it. If Sarah ever wanted to be a spy, she'd have to work on hiding that.

The wife sold Amway, and Sarah said, "I've been meaning to get into that. It sounds like an ideal lifestyle." Then Sarah mouthed to herself, *ideal lifestyle.* I asked her silently, *Who are you?*

The doctor husband was from Iowa—no, Ohio. I ate with one hand in his lap.

As we all headed out together after dinner, the husband said, pointedly, "I'll be in touch about that back problem you mentioned. I'm in Room 407. Four . . . oh . . . seven."

I was careful not to look at the wife, but Sarah stared with her mouth open.

"Tom. Well, I *never,*" hissed the wife. Then she took his arm and they were gone.

"Maybe if you did, he wouldn't," I said.

Sarah's mouth was still open. Then, "Jesus, Maggie. That's rude."

"Sarah. Why do you judge me so much?"

"Someone has to." She adjusted her bra strap. She looked at her rings. She sniffed her wrists, her own perfume.

We returned to the room and Sarah struggled into her nightgown. I changed into a T-shirt. Sarah brushed her hair. I brushed my teeth. We lay down. She fell asleep, as usual, and I didn't, as usual. I never have slept well. Usually I think about things: plan menus, imagine what life would be like if I were a princess, a jockey, a cowboy. Now I just thought about Sarah, sleeping next to me. I thought, this is the person in the world closest to me, genetically. There is nobody more similar to me than her. And nobody I understand less.

THE NEXT day we went shopping at a Caribbean market. Sarah's pink straw hat again, and a matching purse. We walked through the crowded stands ablaze with colors. Turquoise, orange, red, purple, glaring bolts of cloth. Sarah held up something orange and said, "Would Patrick like this? On me?"

I nodded, so she bought it. Afterward, she unfolded it in the sun; it was a sari. Her shoulders sagged, and her lips started trembling. "Why did I just buy this? I'll never wear it." It drooped in her hand, the bright orange tinting her skin yellow. "I can't pull something like this off. He'll just laugh at me." Her face looked like a cracked windshield. She wanted to be a tropical princess. Not a housewife smeared with sunscreen. I felt awful.

"Come on," I said roughly, and grabbed the sari out of her hand. I draped it around her waist, and made her unbuckle her shorts and drop them to the ground. The sari stretched over her legs and curved away in the wind, looking like an enormous slice of cantaloupe.

"There you go. You're beautiful, Sarah." She was, almost. I'm not saying that because she's my sister; I'm saying it despite the fact that she's my sister. Sarah started walking through the market, a little clumsily. I leaned my forehead against a stand and took a deep breath. The inevitables: death, taxes, and family.

After I caught up with her, Sarah started chatting about our great-aunt, our only living relative. Our great-aunt was getting religious, studying the apostles and knowing the names of the saints and what they do. She sent me a St. Jude. This is the woman, who, when I asked if there was a God at age five, had said, "That depends upon your interpretation."

"Last time I visited, she gave me a tract. You know, one of those little pamphlets that say, 'Jesus is your pal!'" Sarah said.

"She told me that I needed a husband."

"You do."

Like I need any more husbands, I thought. "Why do you do that?" I asked.

"What?"

"Decide that your life is great and mine is incomplete just because of Patrick, of all people." I snorted. "Patrick."

"He's a good husband. He provides for me. He's brought many good things to my life."

"Remember your wedding day?" I asked.

I had been her maid of honor. She had a wretched cold, and kept sneezing into her bouquet. I was drunk. Patrick had taken the last-day-of-freedom thing a little too seriously, and was flirting with a bridesmaid from Oklahoma. The bridesmaid kept veering toward Sarah and me, saying, just as if Sarah weren't the bride, "Get that guy *away* from me, cripes."

Sarah was miserable. She looked like an enormous dumpling in a tulle dress that had cost five thousand dollars. She said to me, "I don't think this is such a great idea." I nodded, and pressed Kleenex against her lower eyelids so that she wouldn't mess up her makeup, crying.

Sarah sucked it up, married him quickly, and smiled for all the pictures. I slept with Patrick for the first time three years later.

"He's my husband," Sarah now said.

"Hey," I said. "Did you know that the phrase, 'Always a bridesmaid, never a bride,' originated as a Listerine commercial?"

"Why won't you get married, Maggie?"

I laughed. "To whom?"

Sarah looked down. "It seems like there's always somebody you're seeing."

"Maybe it's too late for me. When everyone was pairing up and getting engaged, I don't know what I was doing. I don't know where I was. I missed it, somehow."

Sarah wanted to hurry back to the boat to eat the buffet lunch and attend the informational video show about the island. I walked her back, then bought a hot dog and moved around the market by myself, watching the tourists try to bargain with the locals.

The doctor husband from dinner approached me and touched my arm, lost. We smiled a lot. He asked if I had seen his wife.

I said that she was probably somewhere on the boat. He agreed. We checked my room first.

*   *   *

I CALLED Patrick from the deserted lounge while Sarah flailed in the yacht pool, taking Intro to Scuba lessons.

"Hey."

"Hey?" Patrick can't tell the difference between our voices, Sarah's and mine.

"It's Maggie. Cruise. With your wife."

"Are you bonding?"

I thought, as I had before, how strange for this man. How strange to think *in-laws* and think *sex*. I took a deep breath and said, "I think we should call it off. You and me."

"What? Are you serious?" He actually laughed.

"Don't you ever feel bad, Patrick?"

"No. You do?"

"Yes. No. But I'm trying to, Patrick. I think that the least I can do is try. You, too." I looked out the window at a small bird flying toward the boat.

"OK." But I knew he wouldn't; that nobody, in the end, would feel bad but Sarah. Then he said, "But you know you'll come crawling back."

Patrick was silent on the line as I watched the bird come closer, then closer, then crash into the window. Its neck twisted and it dropped to the deck, leaving only its own afterimage and a small drop of blood. Patrick was still breathing on the phone, waiting.

THE NEXT day was "Walk-Around Day." No scheduled activities—we were each of us on our own. There were paths, roads, a jungle, everything a tourist could need to get completely lost.

I called my shrink long distance while Sarah was at breakfast, and asked her if she thought I was sick. She said that she's a Freudian—either everyone's sick, or nobody is. I said, "Sarah's

not." Then Sarah showed up at the door. "I'm not what?" she
asked.

"Sick," I said, one hand on the phone.

"I take vitamins," Sarah said. "Let's go."

We disembarked and began our walk, up a road flanked by
jungle on either side. The road dipped and rose and every now
and then we saw ocean, or caught a breeze. There was vegetation. Sarah really cared about the vegetation. I wished we had
brought a pitcher of something.

I thought about the husband the day before, the doctor. At
first he was impotent, so we both lay with one hand behind our
heads as he explained 401k to me. I had never understood it
before, but now I did. I said that it sounded like a very good idea.
He agreed.

After the sex, he talked about my body parts, one by one, as
if they were the Seven Wonders of the World. The thing about
those Seven Wonders, nobody gets to live there. People visit and
send postcards from there to the real places in their lives—
Cleveland, Topeka, the two-bedroom house in Pittsburgh that's
home, after all, because home is where you spend the useless
time in between the exciting events you call your life.

Anyway, he had just done that so I would remember him as
a great lover.

We walked around to the safe side of a wood fence and
rested our arms on top of it, watching the empty road. Sarah's
upper arms creased a little bit. She hiked one foot up on the
lower railing.

"Maggie," Sarah said. "Did you bring someone into our room
yesterday?"

"What? Why? Yes."

"I had a feeling. There was Brut cologne all over the sheets."

"Do you, um, like Brut?"

"Maggie, what's wrong with you? Where did you meet this

guy, in five minutes? Why do you act like that? It's totally disgusting."

"Sarah, you live every situation wondering exactly what Jane Austen would have done." I climbed over the fence and paced on the side of the road.

"How does one become this way, I don't understand." Her fists found her hips and stayed there.

"I'll tell you, Sarah. Things are different for me. I don't know why. I see people with husbands and babies, and it seems so amazing that they managed to pull that off. It seems strange that anyone would have someone to . . . I don't know. To keep their history for them, I guess."

"I'll keep your history, Maggie."

"Hell, Sarah, you don't even know half of my history."

"You're my sister."

A car approached out of nowhere on the empty road, with ribbons and flags sprouting out of the sides. A loudspeaker was attached to the hood, and garbled words were coming out of it. I was still thinking about the word, "sister." The car veered around the curve, and I froze as it aimed straight for me. Sarah's hand magically clutched my shoulder, reaching over the fence and pulling me close to her. The car sped away down the hill and I stared after it.

"Wow. Good reflexes, Sarah." When I turned to her, Sarah's face was white as salt.

"You idiot. You're part of me, forever," Sarah said. "Just like Patrick is part of me, forever. My husband." She looked away as a drumming sound faded in, almost drowning out her last words: "You don't get it."

Approaching from up the road was a whirl of black bodies, all running toward us in shorts, bare chests and sneakers. It was a race. They were sprinting downhill. It must have been the final stretch. The feet in unison sounded like thunder. There were so

many men that they blurred together, until they were just one
body, running fast, their sweat gleaming on their skin.

They were beside us. For a second, I couldn't tell who was
moving—them or me. It felt like they were running into me,
their bodies washing through me like dark water or wine, leaving me a little different for the duration. And then they were
gone, and there I was again, on the sidelines, hand on the fence.

Sarah was still looking at me. All of a sudden, I knew that
she knew about Patrick. She had always known. I knew this the
way that she knew. How you just do, when you're sisters.

For the first time since I was a small child, I was scared.

"I'm sorry," I whispered. "It's over now. Sorry."

"God damn it."

"I'm so sorry." I covered my mouth with my hand and talked
through it. "Sarah. I'm so sorry."

"Why, Maggie?" Sarah's face was turned toward me, as if
someone were holding her chin in place, forcing her to look. Her
face fell into a million pieces. But she stood there, and I realized
that, even though I was older, she was the bigger, stronger one.
She could break me.

She reached one arm across the fence and I closed my eyes.
Then I felt the weight of the hand that could have reached for
my throat, but chose instead to rest on my shoulder.

"I don't understand, Maggie." She was crying, hard, the way
I used to. "You all just run, and run, and run."

We turned away from each other, two sisters. Still crying,
Sarah looked uphill at the trees, the road turning upon itself like
a snake. I looked downhill at the fading backs of the men, running as if they would explode, toward whatever line they had
drawn in the sand to call it the end.

The Fast

———

Peel me a grape.

—Mae West

Janet went on a fast, although it wasn't Yom Kippur and she's only half Jewish anyway. She just stopped eating at sundown, in the middle of a cheeseburger. She let it drop from her fingers and stared at the pinkish ketchup soaking into the bun. The pickle sliding off the patty toward the plate but never making it there.

Janet looked out the window at the glare of the sun, now hidden behind the mountains. She thought, give yourself some time.

But there had been time, and men. A Transcendentalist who told her he could fly. It was more like hopping, he said. An urban planner who said that he had named all his unborn children in advance, German names like Franz and Wolfgang. "So girls can call him Wolf," he had explained. A poet who rhymed "loss" with "albatross." A man named Barkey Clarke.

A divorcee with Garanimals labels sewn into the inside hems of his clothes. He said it was convenient, really, that way he knew that the giraffe shirts would match the giraffe pants, etc. His ex-wife did this for him the first year they were married, so he wouldn't wake her up at six A.M. asking, "Honey? Does this match?"

So Janet stopped eating, mid-chew. It was nearly Christmas. She had spent the last Christmas in Alabama, with Nicholas's parents. Nicholas had really loved her then, especially when she choked down black-eyed peas to please his mother. "I like a girl who can put it away," his mother had said to Nicholas, and he had given Janet the most beautiful smile. She had smiled back, peas in her teeth. In Alabama, mistletoe grows way up high in the trees. To get it down, you have to shoot it with a shotgun.

THE SECOND day of the fast, Janet stared out the window for two hours at work. It was snowing. The traffic sounds slowed and hushed. When her boss asked her about the report she was supposed to be writing, Janet held up one finger. "Shhhh," she said. He stopped talking and cocked his head to one side. They listened together to the hum of office machines and the crunch of fresh snow meeting tires. Then her boss lowered his eyebrows and went away.

Walking home that evening, Janet cut through the yard of an apartment complex. She heard giggling from above. Two kids on the balcony retreated and slid out of the streetlamp's light. Janet looked at her feet, then crouched down to see better. A dry carrot lay in the snow, with red yarn tied around it. The line of yarn stretched from the carrot all the way up to the hidden fingers of the children on the second floor.

"What are you trying to catch?" Janet called up to them. "Hey." They appeared again. After a long pause, the bigger one finally answered, "A rabbit. A white one."

Once Janet caught a fish, its mouth opening and closing, wriggling in her hands. She didn't feel sorry for it. She didn't feel hungry for it, either. She wondered what it would be like for humans, to be caught like that. She imagined taking a bite out of a burrito on the street and suddenly being submerged in water, a big halibut gripping her in its slimy fin and hollering in fish language.

That night, Janet dreamt that she had moved to a new apartment, which was in actuality an enormous turkey carcass. She lived inside the chest cavity. It was dim, but dinner was always ready if you had the stomach to peel it off the walls. Janet tried to poke windows between the ribs. She hung curtains and wondered if they would get grease stains.

She then dreamt that she was back with Nicholas. He was wearing a kaftan. He pointed to different women, saying, "I want that one and that one and that one . . ."

Janet woke up after this dream, sat up and pulled the covers to her chest. The night sky had an orange tint from the reflection of lights off the snow.

She got out of bed and turned on the light. Squinting, she walked to the bathroom and looked in the mirror. She looked all right, except for her shoulders and her waist and her nose and her neck. Why, why, why, why, why, she asked herself. He left me why, why, why, why, why?

It was cold, so she turned the light off and slipped back under the covers. She thought about *Siddhartha*, how it was the only book Nicholas had read during the entire year they were together. Siddhartha had fasted to find Enlightenment. If Janet recalled correctly, this tactical move didn't get him Enlightenment, but it did land him a job selling produce and dry goods. Nicholas had once said, "Enlightenment is the sound of a machine gun going, 'Buddha-buddha-buddha-buddha.'"

Janet wrapped her arms around her legs. She waited until she felt that quiet place inside her, and then lay back down. It was morning before she slept again.

THE THIRD day of the fast was more productive, although Janet forgot where she put things. All day she kept retrieving her Coke can from the copy machine, her memos from the lunchroom. Her feet from the top of her desk.

Janet craved salt, so she drank bouillon and wondered if it

counted as food. Then she realized that coffee wasn't food since it had no calories. She thought of the other things that weren't food. Water. Velveeta. She had heard somewhere that, before they mix in the yellow food coloring, Velveeta is actually clear. Food isn't clear.

Janet's boss hovered around her desk. Janet asked, "May I help you?"

He asked, "Is something going on? Janet?"

But she was already looking out the window again.

He shook her shoulder. "*Janet.*"

She turned to him. "Is the shoulder a sexual harassment zone?"

Her boss backed away, palms facing front, fingers spread wide.

"I was just wondering," Janet said.

At five o'clock, Janet waited at the front door for the other people in the office to put on their coats. Her office had signed up for ice skating lessons as a pod, at a rink a few blocks away. Janet walked there with the other participants: several fern-waterers like herself, and her boss, who was showing some kind of sporting spirit. He joked around with everyone and they laughed uproariously at everything he said, just because he made three times their salaries. Janet hid her face in the neck of her coat.

Classes were to be taught by a seventy-one-year-old ex–Ice Capades star named Lillie. Lillie had the moves, gliding in a hot pink outfit and nylons that puckered at her knees. Lillie showed them the arabesque. Janet's boss threw one leg into the air, arms spread wide like an airplane. He smiled at everyone. Janet pulled her hat down further and concentrated on keeping her ankles from wobbling.

Working around the edge of the rink, Janet thought she was doing OK, staying upright mostly without holding on very much to the rail. Her skates were dull and one scudded behind.

She smiled at the other people on the ice, while lifting and lowering her feet, clomping more than skating and occasionally contorting at the waist and waving her arms like windmills. Every time Janet felt a little secure, the former Ice Capades star would whiz by, whumping her on the back and yelling in her ear, "Edges! Edges!" And Janet would fall down.

Janet sat on the bleachers as everyone drifted around the ice. Her authority figure and her colleagues, all clutching at each other and trying to throw limbs into graceful poses while moving forward at relatively high speeds. Can I bear this? she thought. No. Nobody can bear this. Janet stomped off the rink, put on normal shoes and started for home.

She walked all the way to her old apartment before realizing that she didn't live there anymore. She hadn't done this in months. Once there, she bummed a cigarette from a man who was sitting on a bench. She leaned against a pole and smoked. This, smoking, is what people do instead of eating, she thought. In college, I did this instead of eating.

Janet had lived in this apartment building for years, until Nicholas moved in with her. They lived together for four months. Then he moved out. And then Janet moved out.

But those four months. Nicholas would sneak out every Sunday morning before Janet woke up and come back with the *New York Times* and bagels. He took out the garbage. He kissed the tip of her braid, where the rubber band was. His skin scented the apartment until Janet realized that she'd never be able to get it out of the curtains, the carpet.

Janet now watched a couple moving into the apartment building, grunting up the stairs in the dark. They carried an enormous couch of indistinguishable color. They were struggling up the bends in the stairs when the girl dropped her end and said, "Ouch," loudly. The couch thudded against the wood and the boy winced. Then he lowered his end and hurried over to inspect his girlfriend's hand. She pushed her hair behind her ears with her good hand. They quietly talked together over the hurt hand like it was a child, their first. Janet watched, and then, looking down, she found herself in the same pose as that girl, one hand crumpled in the palm of the other.

ON THE FOURTH day, Janet still hadn't forgiven anyone. And aside from some insights on the Theory of Relativity (she finally got it), she hadn't reached Enlightenment. She was crabby and snapped at her boss at work, telling him that she could do his job with one brain tied behind her back.

He called her into his office. "What the hell is wrong with you?" he asked.

Janet just frowned at him. He was three years younger than she was.

"I'm not eating," she finally said.

"Stress? Problems at home?"

"I'm just not eating. I've stopped. I think I'm done with it."

"Done?" His brow wrinkled up like a raisin.

"Yeah. I don't think I really need to do it anymore. I think I've got this whole food thing licked."

"Licked." Her boss tapped his pencil against his desk.

Janet looked him in the eyes. This is fun, she realized. She said, very seriously, "I'm immortal."

Her boss licked his lips. Janet knew that he liked her. Janet knew that he was regretting this fact right now. He walked away, out of his own office, and didn't come back. Janet sat in the chair next to the desk. She put her head down on the cool wood surface.

When she was a child, she had wanted to be a newscaster, except with hair that moved. Current Events was her favorite class. One week, she cut a story out of the newspaper and read it to the class, about a woman who had an old beehive hairdo, but she never washed it or brushed it because she was homeless.

Bugs crawled inside and laid eggs in that hive, warmed by her scalp and protected from the wind and street grime. Janet imagined that it felt like a real hive.

The eggs hatched. Hungry maggots fed on the carbon from her head. Eventually, they made their way to her brain. They ate that and she died.

The teacher sent a note home to Janet's mother. The week before, Janet had read a story to the class about a young woman who ate herself to death. This was before they had a name for bulimia. The young woman had starved herself for a week, then she opened the refrigerator and ate straight out of it, standing. Three pounds of cheese, two pounds of raw hamburger, a loaf of bread, carrots, a half gallon of milk, a jar of applesauce, a coffeecake, an orange, unpeeled . . . these are the things the doctors found in her stomach after they opened it. Some of the food was still in her dead throat, trying to travel downward.

THE EVENING of the fifth day was Christmas Eve. Janet walked to her favorite coffee shop in the snow, looking at the lights and thinking they looked like neon lollipops. She stepped inside and the man at the counter snarled, "Wish me a Merry Christmas and I put arsenic in your coffee."

Absorbed in carrying her latte without spilling onto her fleece gloves, Janet almost butted into someone. She looked up. It was Nicholas. She met his face with terror. He stared at her like a startled cat. Janet hadn't seen him since he left her six months ago. He was wearing tights.

A woman was with him, the same woman he had left her for, Janet assumed. Janet could see why—black curly hair and perfect makeup, the kind that men think is just natural color. They say, "My girlfriend never wears makeup," until they move in together, and then they shut up about it.

Nicholas said, "Janet."

Janet said, "Nicholas."

The girlfriend said, "Oh, *please*."

Janet looked at the girlfriend. Her hand was tucked into Nicholas's jacket pocket. Nicholas pulled at his earring, tilting his head in that way that men do.

After a short silence, the girlfriend said, "Well, this was fun, but we'll be late for my parents."

Nicholas had never met Janet's parents. Janet looked up at his face. He looked dashing, with dark circles under his eyes. He reached out toward her and Janet braced herself, but he just steadied her drink, which was beginning to tilt and spill. Then he gave Janet a look she couldn't comprehend, so she blurted, "I'm fasting."

Nicholas said, "Oh yeah? For how long?"

"Five days."

"But you're drinking a latte."

Janet looked at the cup in her hand. "It's liquid." She covered it with a plastic lid.

"But it's food."

"Why?"

"Milk."

"Well, you need something."

The girlfriend had already turned to leave. "Come *on*," she said. Nicholas followed her through the café, glancing back just once at Janet.

Janet took a deep breath and pulled on her coat. "No big deal," she said into her turtleneck as she opened the door and stepped outside. The snow had the consistency of the insides of apples. She wrapped her scarf twice around her neck and was about to start the walk home when she saw Nicholas across the street, on his knees. Then standing, dusting himself free of snow and following his girlfriend, who was squeaking away in her Sorels.

Nicholas caught up to his girlfriend. He tried to touch her shoulder. His hand slid off her parka. He patted her shoulder again, and the girlfriend whirled. She quickly slapped him in the face.

Her arm stuck in the air after the slap, the noise rebounding across the snow. It sounded like the pop of a single kernel of popcorn.

Janet stared as they both trudged away, post-slap, Nicholas following his girlfriend by a couple of yards. They unlocked the doors of a white car, got in and stared straight ahead. Their heads didn't move, silhouetted by a street lamp. The brakes lit once, violently. Then nothing, just a cold car and the quiet figures within.

After she got a little numb standing there and watching, Janet started walking home again, her breath shooting out in clouds. Then she suddenly veered into a pizza place. The heat instantly warmed her face as she opened the doors. It was bright and smelled like grease and warm skin. She walked up to the counter, pulled crumpled bills out of her pocket and ordered a whole pie with green olives and anchovies.

She sat down in a wood booth, waiting for the pizza to cook. She looked out of the window. The car was still there. Janet folded one hand over her flat stomach. She tapped a Christmas carol with the fingers of her other hand—"The Twelve Days of Christmas." Janet remembered what she had given Nicholas for Christmas last year—a pig that oinked "Jingle Bells" when punched. She smiled.

Her appetite was back.

Via Texas

———

I'm going to give you
a little inside information—
I'm going to leave you the
first chance I get.

—Mae West

At first it's too bright. Then your eyes adjust like a camera, you point them in every direction. You don't miss anything, not the sand pushed into the breeze, not the broken bottle of gin on the side of the road. Rabbits cross in front of the tires. Maybe it's for the rush of air from the rented Renault Alliance you have named Frieda. No air-conditioning, no antifreeze, but it's red. You wave past the brush, in the hot noon with your name on it, your kiss good-bye on its cracked lips.

Push the visor so that you can squint out, so you can damn the red plastic sunglasses you bought at the last gas station thirty miles ago. Throw them out the window and wonder who will someday find them twisted in the road, here, way out in East Jesus. That person will wonder at their story, when there is no story, they were just cheap.

You throw the next logical thing out the window, your wallet. Then you stomp on the brakes and say, "Crazy, crazy, crazy," as you back up to where you think you were. You open the car door and there it is, the wallet, right there in the dust where your foot is stepping. "Crazy," you say again.

When you were young, your hair was blond and cut straight across your forehead in bangs. You carried around a plastic starfish and a flowered stuffed hippo named "Hippie." Your mother called you "sweet pea" or sometimes "pea" for short.

You were going to be a firewoman when you grew up, and save buildings and the people who lived in them. You asked for a Dalmatian. You didn't get one, so you painted spots on your cat. You sang, "This Land Is My Land, This Land Is My Land."

Now you are leaving a man who says that all love is conditional. He'll find his dirty dishes left in the sink and his birthday gift delivered in advance. He'll call your mother a bitch on the telephone.

He'll destroy everything else you left behind: your radio, sheets, the frozen eggplant casserole, the painting of a goldfish that you gave him for his thirty-third birthday. He'll slash your clothes with a steak knife. He'll put these things in cardboard boxes to show you when you come home. He'll call your mother again, this time to ask her to ask you to come home.

You are leaving Texas but you are still in Texas. You are leaving Texas via Texas, which is no quick way, but the only way to leave Texas.

The air is hot as you stick your arm out the window, shimmying the wheel with your other hand. You see yourself in the rearview mirror, your dull hair waving around your face. You look at your chin and mouth, you look at your eyebrows. You imagine yourself in a movie, and wonder what would happen next. A new scene, or maybe a flashback? You light a cigarette and see that you are staying in character. Every breath you take is supposed to happen. You can't miss.

What I Wore

------

*"Goodness, what
diamonds."*

*"Goodness had nothing to
do with it, dearie."*

—Mae West

I left Jerry the same day I auditioned for the role of a boysen-berry in a yogurt commercial. I had never seen a boysenberry, so I wasn't very convincing. But I had left men before, and I nearly even convinced myself.

For the leaving part, I teased my hair to look like a coed from the '50s caught in a tornado. I named the hairstyle "What *Really* Happened to the Feminine Mystique." I wore a gray turtleneck with a miniskirt and a green corduroy jacket with leather patches at the elbows. Wool tights and snakeskin cow-boy boots. I was trying for sexy, distraught, and pathetic.

Jerry and I packed my truck with all the breakable objects. Only the solid, clunky things were left in the apartment—wood chairs, sofa, crocheted Afghan, tool set. I dumped everything from ceramic bowls into plastic bags and paper sacks, to be picked through later. We went to a bar for dinner, my last meal with him. I ate a squeaky chicken sandwich with a tomato slice that kept sliding around until I gave up.

As we were leaving, I asked Jerry for a quarter and slid it into a toy machine in the lobby. When I turned the handle, out dropped a rubber ball, red and yellow like a Technicolor globe. I bounced it on the icy street and then put it in the pocket of my coat. Which is where I would find it months later, sur-rounded by hard, crumpled Kleenex that had once been wet with sobbing as I gunned the truck through the dark, icy roads.

At my new apartment, I pulled the truck over and cut the engine. I watched the hazard lights beat against the snow in perfect time with the words to "New York, New York," which were sounding in my head although I lived in Denver. By the time I left the truck and walked up to my new front door, my fists were so clenched with cold, I couldn't recognize them.

I DID TEMP work those days, and left the office at random times for acting auditions. I wore my respective audition outfits to the office. Even when I worked in the same place for a week or so, the office personnel thought I was a different temp in each new outfit. For the part of a mom in a commercial for bedroom furniture, I wore a light blue linen dress. For the bitch role in a local action-adventure movie, stilettos and a gun.

When there was no audition, I played the role of office girl. There were closets that only I could enter. Staples and staplers that only I could dispense. This is no time for a woman of adventure, I would tell myself and begin a mail merge.

But nighttimes were different. I was rehearsing as Anita, a drug addict and slut in a play called *But What about Me,* a production in a small theater. The drug addiction made the character complex. Anita came from Vidalia, Georgia, the onion capital of the world, and I would practice my accent during the day at work until I felt like I, too, had lived in Georgia.

Sometimes when I went to a party, I'd slip into Anita's accent, her memories even. At one bash, I started making up a story about a time when I woke up after a night of multicolored drugs. How I didn't remember how I got there, didn't know where I was. "What state, even," I said. In the rented hotel room of an architect from Kentucky, next to some train tracks. "Two broken, yes, *broken* condoms on the floor, no note, no train fare. Clothes gone, I'm naked except for one sock. I'm thinking, How did I get here? I'm thinking, Where is Bruce? Not his real name."

Someone interrupted. "What *was* his real name?"

"What's *your* name?" I asked him.

Someone laughed, and the story was over. Thank God, I thought. But it didn't stop me from doing it again, later, at another party, then at a dinner. Then to my friends, who were as pleased as I was at my suddenly wild life.

"YOU KNOW what you are? You're a *cowboy*."

"No, like this: 'Y'know whady'are? Yurra cowboy,'" said Kevin, the director.

I frowned. "Don't tell me how to speak."

"But you're supposed to be wasted."

"I know, but don't tell me how to *talk*. Give me *direction*."

"Okay. Act wasted. Directly."

"This is how wasted people act. They try to act sober."

"Well, do something." He crossed his arms. "Do something that indicates you're stoned. Do something stupid."

"You're a great guy," I said and took a drink of water. My shoulders ached and my head hurt.

"Did it ever occur to you that what's wrong here is sexual tension?"

"Between us?" I asked, surprised.

"No. Between you and yourself. There just isn't any."

"In my role?"

"In your role."

"So I'm supposed to want myself?"

"It would help," he said.

So I tried it. "You know what y'are? You're a cowboy." I put my hands on my hips, then lower, then higher. My fingernails scraped the fabric and tugged on the front of my gray dress.

"Much better," Kevin said.

After rehearsal, he took me out to a late dinner. A raw oyster slipped from its shell and landed flush on the right breast of my dress. He stared, then said, "I feel like a zoom lens. Sorry. Let me help you."

He offered his napkin. Instead of taking it from his hand, I poked out my chest. He refolded the napkin so that his fingers wouldn't touch the fabric, and wiped off my dress.

I didn't say anything but ate another oyster, sucking at the shell while Kevin wondered if he had acted like a prude. When a cracked piece of calcium slid onto my tongue, I swallowed it whole so he wouldn't hear the crunch on my teeth. I felt the little shell travel all the way down my throat until it hit the place where there are no more nerves.

I had seen love in the surrender scenes in movies, the women swooning in their red dresses and the men catching them. When the truth is, you can confuse the two, you can think it's love but it's only surrender. Actually, most people wet their pants when they swoon. Most people swoon when they're wearing anything but a red dress. The last time I swooned, I didn't—I passed out. I was wearing a T-shirt ripped from the argument I had gotten into with my then-boyfriend, and cotton underwear with purple flowers scattered over it like a rash. I had woken up on the bathroom floor, stood and walked back to my bedroom, all by myself.

I looked at Kevin, an average man, then poured the dregs of my martini out of the shaker. I pulled at a run in my stocking and watched it shoot up my thigh like a hand. Kevin smiled because I was a sure thing. Or at least, a thing. We were leaving. I gathered my jacket around my shoulders before I remembered my stain. I made sure that it showed, wet and gleaming on the fabric like a mother's brooch.

A WEEK LATER, I went on a date with a man I met at a temp job. I said yes because when I coughed, he held his own fist to his chest and said, "Excuse me." He continued on with a story about his dog, and I was fascinated that he couldn't tell the difference between us.

He showed up in a white jacket, blue shirt, and red tie. I was wearing a black dress and a hat with plastic flowers glued on.

"You look like a dentist," I said.

"You look like a voodoo princess," he said.

He decided to take me to a movie. He said, "You'll like a movie, because you're an actress."

I said, "I'll like a movie, because I'm a human being."

"That too," he said.

It was a story about a woman and a man. The man blew up many things and shot people. The woman had a drinking problem that was suddenly cured when she was taken hostage.

The week before, I had auditioned for a similar role in an independent film. Actually, the role was completely different, more along the lines of *La Femme Nikita*. But the clothes were the same.

I was trying out for everything those days, squeezing auditions between commercials, temp jobs, and rehearsals for *But What about Me*. The director for this film was staying downtown in the Brown Palace. When I asked at the front desk for the director's room, I'm sure they thought I was a prostitute, with my shiny black shoestring dress and false eyelashes.

During the audition, I played three scenes on camera. For one of them, I had to pretend to shoot eleven people. For another, I had to confess to a nun. For the last one, I had to sit on a toilet, white panties lacing my ankles, softly singing "Tainted Love."

I told my date about the audition as we left the movie theater and walked into a bar next door. "I didn't get the part, I'm sure."

"How do you know?"

"They kept commenting about my nose. How it's not a brutal nose, it's more of a sweet nose."

"Well, you look so innocent." I made a face and he backpedaled, "Perhaps you do."

"I hate when people say that. Because then if you don't act innocent, it's a big surprise. Like you're always supposed to be the ingenue or something."

"What parts do you get cast for?"

"Well, the ingenue. No, really, teddy bears and pieces of fruit. Usually commercials. Sometimes a college kid in a made-for-TV special, because I look so young."

"And this is satisfying to you?"

"You have to look at the bigger picture."

He was an actuary. Apparently, he was the youngest actuary at his level in the United States. There are different levels. He testifies in court a lot.

He talked about his ex-wife. "I should have known that we had boundary problems when we started wearing each other's socks."

"I left my boyfriend because he called me his girlfriend so much, I nearly forgot my own name. Jerry's girlfriend."

"Been there. Ann's husband."

"And then you dress the way they want you to."

"Let them cut your hair."

"I said 'we' all the time, instead of 'I.'"

"How about when you go to the grocery store and then look down at the cart and think, I don't even *like* cornflakes. I don't like most of this stuff. But you don't put it back on the shelves," he said.

"Yeah."

It should have been intimate and friendly, but I started to see myself in everything he did—the way he lifted his glass, smiled at me after he swallowed. The way he dug his fingernails into his palm. I realized that all evening he had never given me a differing opinion; never said anything I wouldn't have said myself.

I told him that I was tired, but I wasn't. I was having a lot of trouble breathing. When I got out of my chair, I felt like I was walking on sand.

As soon as I got home, I called my friend with the strongest opinions on everything, and asked her if she thought John F. Kennedy was a great president in spite of the Cuban Missile Crisis and the Bay of Pigs. I slumped against the wall while she talked. As her voice rose in conviction, the one in my head grew quiet until I could breathe easily again.

ON OPENING night for *But What about Me,* I took speed and Valium. I had never done hard drugs before, but I thought it might help with my character. It did. I hit all my lines right on. Oh yeah, I thought. This is it. This is really her. She's me. We're each other.

The audience loved the sex scenes, the drug scenes, and especially the sex and drug scenes. At intermission, the leading man pulled me behind a curtain. He said, "You're on fire."

I let him press against me in my black coat, already saturated with sweat from the hot lights. He whispered, "What are you like? Really? Who are you like?"

In the second act, during the scene where I was supposed to hit the couch with a baseball bat, I missed and hit the TV instead. The glass broke and the plastic dented. So I figured what the hell and kept going at it. It wasn't very satisfying after the first crash, not as good as I thought it would be. Mostly because it wasn't really breaking, just denting and leaning and cracking. I hit it each time as if it was the first, as if you could get that feeling back again.

When I had finished, when there wasn't one bit of glass or tubing or plastic that wasn't altered, I looked up. Kevin the director had his face in his hands. It was his television set. The leading man just stared at me. We were supposed to kiss next,

or something. I forgot what I was doing. I forgot who I was supposed to be. Dizzy, I stared at Kevin in the wings. "Line," I said.
"Line, motherfucker."

AFTER THE play had been running for three weeks, Jerry called
and asked me when I would be through with this foolishness.
"Come on home," he said.

"I am home." I looked around my studio apartment. Clothes
were scattered on the floor and there were piles of makeup by
the full-length mirror.

"How's work?" he asked.

I talked about my temp jobs, because I knew that was what
he meant—not acting. It made him feel better if he could feel
sorry for me. So I told him about my last supervisor, who taught
me how to count. "The first one is *one*, the second one is *two*,
the third one is *three* . . ." I told him about the job where I had
to wear a name tag that said, simply, "Temp."

Jerry talked about his father's business, and how everyone
missed me. He said that when people asked what I was doing he
always said, "Making the biggest mistake of her life."

I heard a rustling sound on the phone and asked him what
he was doing. "Hanging pants," he said. The thought of Jerry's
slack pants on their hangers made me feel a sudden vast ten-
derness for him. But then he said, "After you're done being the
spokesmodel for the monster truck bash at Five Points, you're
going to come back for me and I'll have moved on."

"I'm trying to do something real here."

"What's real about media?"

Before I hung up he said, "Come home" once more. I heard
it all the time in my head. Sometimes when I was alone in the
bathroom, I sat on the fuzzy toilet seat cover and silently justi-
fied myself to him. Often I spoke aloud, complete with gestures,
enumerating my accomplishments to the mirror until it seemed

like I was talking about someone else. Occasionally I impro-
vised and made up feats of talent and bravery until I really was
describing someone else. That felt a little better.

"I'M NOT AN actor," I said to my acting coach. "I can barely do
a convincing impression of myself."

"Who's asking you to be yourself? Nobody."

"Maybe that's the problem," I said dramatically. I was hun-
gover, and didn't care what she thought of me that day.

"This is a business," she said. "You're a product. If you want
to be a person, go do something else."

"Like what?"

"Exactly." I glared at her. "This isn't Hollywood," she said.
"This is Denver. These are J.C. Penney's commercials and one-
act plays we're talking about. Think of what's at stake here.
You're doing this because you have nothing else."

"I can type like a sonofabitch."

"Then go type." She grabbed her coffee cup and stood up.

"No, I'm sorry. I'm tired."

"Get out of here."

That night, I had a few drinks and took some pills someone
handed me in the bathroom.

I walked up to an attractive, slightly balding man at the bar.
I tapped him on the arm until he turned around. His face was
polite and intelligent above his Armani suit. I said clearly and
distinctly, "You know what you are? You're a *cow*boy."

Then I started feeling sick, like my heart was about to gallop
down the bar, drop off the edge and thump on the ground until
someone stepped on it. I don't remember what else happened
there, but for a while I thought I was doing the cha-cha with Jeff
Goldblum. I remember asking the bartender, "If Picasso painted
a flounder, what would it look like?" Then I was mad at myself
because I had been saving that line for a more educated audience.

My friend Katya grabbed my forearm. "What did you take?"

I said, "I can take it. I can take it all." She rolled her eyes.

My skirt had tiny bells all along the waistband, so every step I took created a sleigh of jingles. By the time I found myself home in my apartment, the jingles sounded like the telephone. I couldn't tell the difference, so I kept pulling myself off the mattress and crawling across the carpet to my own jingling, muttering, "I'm coming, I'm coming."

After I picked up the telephone for the third time and listened to the dial tone, I made my way to the couch. Someone was calling but didn't want to talk to me, I was sure. Then I wasn't so sure. That's when I realized for the first time, head lolling against the woven couch covers, that I had absolutely no idea what I was doing.

Katya called the next morning and reconstructed the night for me.

"I finally found you in a bathroom stall. Between your crying and the jingling noises, you sounded like Tinkerbell dying. After I told you that, you kept saying, 'Clap if you believe!'"

I remembered that she had crawled under the stall and pulled me home, talking about drinks of water and a good long rest from this craziness. She said, "You can't do this again." The whole way back, I kept tripping over the hem of my skirt and thinking that the world was getting too short for me to walk on anymore.

I STOPPED at a red light on Market and Fifteenth, waiting to turn left. The steam was blowing out of the potholes as usual, and I looked great in a black miniskirt, tights, and a soft cream-colored blouse, tucked in. I was a modern girl, lipstick still stuck to my lips from a botched audition.

I saw a familiar dented Nissan in the next lane. Jerry was there, looking at my face in the glare of the window. His hair was long and in ringlets, just like it had been when I met him. He rolled down the window, and I reached over to roll mine down on the passenger side, the seat belt cutting at my hip. He said, "Hi, baby," the way he did when he first loved me. His voice was low, cutting through the traffic sounds and smog. The one place where I could be sure of myself, lodged in another person's voice.

He said, "I missed your play."

I said, "So did I." The light changed and we drove off in separate directions.

But What about Me closed two weeks early because ticket sales weren't meeting costs. I tried harder, but nobody was very interested no matter what I did, how I played it. Once I imitated Jodie Foster in my delivery style. Then I tried Kristy McNichol, Susan Sarandan, even Diane Wiest. Sissy Spacek was slightly better, but not much. I blamed the script.

For the first couple of weeks of the show, I had started doing speed regularly to make the character authentic. It helped at first. Then I took it just so I could drag myself onstage. I didn't sleep at all the last three days of the show.

On closing night the assistant director said, "Here, some guy gave these to you." He handed me an armful of white tulips. There was a small card with a scribbled *I love you.* Unsigned. I was exhausted. I smiled and thanked him, accidentally stumbled into the curtain, then toward the dressing room. I looked at my reflection in the brightly lit mirror and sank into my Naugahyde chair. I was still in costume, which was a gigantic black overcoat with nothing underneath. I floated inside like a parachuted child. I thought, Oh yes, please love me, whoever we are.

The plaster walls suddenly bent, the way a mermaid bends at the waist to change direction. I laid my head down on the dressing table. The paramedics came, after the entire cast took turns trying to shake me awake.

Two days later in the psych ward of the hospital, Kevin sat next to me for a long time. I picked at the sheet.

I said, "Don't feel responsible."

"I don't. You have problems."

"I know. You think you have to tell me? I'm in a hospital."

"Were you doing drugs when I cast you in this role?"

I was interested. "Did you think I was?"

"I thought maybe."

I took this as a sign of my talent until he reconsidered and said, "No, not really."

I put my hand on his arm. "I just thought the drugs might help. With the role. With my life. Maybe the role would help me with my life."

"It's not as easy as that. You are *not* what you eat," he said.

It's been three years since I quit acting, and when I tell my new kind lover about those times, he is good-natured with me, as if I used to be a hooker, or a lawyer.

"But that's all a part of what you're trying to be now," he says.

"A part of what?" I ask.

"You."

"Me? What? What part?" I ask him. "Who?"

THE THEME of my very first play was Animals at the Zoo. I was in first grade, and I played a chameleon. My costume had a long, white tail. The teacher had instructed the sixth grade lighting crew to change the color of the spotlight from green to blue to red as I spoke my one line.

My line was difficult, all the more so because it was short: "I am a chameleon—I change my identity to match my environment."

This sentence made little sense to me, even when my sister said, "It means you change colors depending on where you stand." To me, there were three big words and two My's, and I had to remember what went where. At night I practiced the sentence by the glow of the nightlight. "I change my identity to match my environment."

The day of the pageant, I was hysterical. "What if I forget? What if I forget?" I was almost crying as my sister rolled her eyes and put on her costume. She was a princess, with lipstick cheeks and a purple satin hair band. I was jealous—she got to be royalty while I had to be some weird animal. My mother made hot milk and honey to soothe me, but it only made me sleepy and anxious.

Finally, my mother pulled a felt tip marker from a drawer in the kitchen and wrote the words on my right palm, spelling them phonetically.

Ka me le on

I den ti te

En vi ro ment

If I forgot, she said, I could just sound out the words on my hand.

I can't remember the details of how I got to school, how I stepped into my pilly costume or pulled the cotton mask over my head. But I'll always remember the stage lights like warm fingers on my small shoulders and arms. I walked to the center of the stage and shouted (our teacher had told us to speak loudly):

"I am a chameleon. I change . . ."

Then I forgot everything. I looked at my teacher, who was quickly mouthing the words in a silent babble. I turned my head to look at my hand, but the mask had suddenly shifted and the eyeholes were roaming around my forehead and sweaty hair.

Now my memory shifts so that I see myself from the back only, staring into the black hole of an audience. My costume was pajamas with feet. My mask, a pillowcase with rubber bands securing little knobs in a chameleon-like ridge down the back.

I pulled off the mask. It dangled from my fingers and dropped to the stage floor. The green spotlight shone on the straight part dividing my braids in two as I looked out at the people in the auditorium. I saw nothing on their faces.

"Identity," I said, palm out in supplication.

It's a word I still wear on my hand.

Erika Krouse's fiction has appeared in *The Atlantic Monthly, Story, Ploughshares, Shenandoah* and *The New Yorker.* She has received scholarships to the Bread Loaf Writer's Conference and the Sewanee Writer's Conference. She currently lives in Boulder, Colorado. *Come Up and See Me Sometime* is her first book.